Glen Willow Gardens

Glen Willow Gardens

Lisa Julin Sharon

GusGus Press • Bedazzled Ink Publishing
Fairfield, California

978-1-949290-05-9 paperback

Cover Design
by

GusGus Press
a division of
Bedazzled Ink Publishing Company
Fairfield, California
http://www.bedazzledink.com

In loving memory of Marguerite and Jane

THE LAST THING I remember before finding myself at Glen Willow Gardens is sitting high up in the cab of a truck with a man who smells of oil and is telling me about his grandson and a great, big fish they caught, while a mutt smiles down at me from a photo over the visor. I remember a ham sandwich, a boy in a long red dress, tilting rows of corn, scolding crows, and sirens.

That's what I tell the psychiatrist and my husband, Hector. No, I don't remember how I happened to be in the truck, and no, I don't know where we were going.

IT WASN'T UNTIL two days after the accident that I was moved from the hospital and found myself waking at Glen Willow Gardens needing to go to the bathroom. I tried to sit up to get out of bed but I was hit with a knife-like pain in my ribs and my right leg and arm didn't seem to be working right.

"Hector," I called out, but my voice was so weak I could hardly hear myself. "Hector!" I called more loudly, then groaned at the pain in my ribs. Still he didn't come. I lay back and stared at the ceiling. Then I looked around. When had Hector changed the wallpaper in my bedroom? He should have at least checked with me first. I would never have chosen pink stripes.

The pressure on my bladder was becoming fierce and I couldn't hold on any longer. I felt the warmth seeping under my bottom.

A round black woman in a light blue smock and pink plastic shoes walked into my room as if she lived there. "How'ya doing Alma? You finally awake?"

I stared at her. Had Hector hired a new cleaning lady?

She came over to my bed and said, "It's almost lunchtime. Turkey with gravy today."

"Where's Hector?" I said.

"Your husband? He's out in the hall. I'll get him."

I watched while she folded a blanket at the end of my bed. I didn't recognize the blanket either. I didn't want Hector to come in while I lay in a puddle of my own pee.

"I've wet myself," I said quietly, hoping she wouldn't hear me.

"Huh?"

"I've wet myself."

"Okay, then. Stay put." She went over to the door and called out, "Connie, come help me with Alma. Bring the wheelchair."

A young woman with hoop earrings and a deep tan came into my room, pushing an empty wheelchair.

"We're going to help you up out of bed," the black woman said. She wore a plastic name tag with a teddy bear smiling on the end and the name "Hattie" in bold letters. Hattie pulled my legs off the bed then she and the other girl hooked their arms under mine, lifted me off the bed, and shifted me over to the wheelchair. All the time I moaned, "Oh, oh, oh," and Hattie said, "You got a cracked rib, honey. Can't do much about it 'cept wait for it to heal up. I'll get you some Tylenol after we're done here."

"I want Hector," I gasped.

"Wheel her into the bathroom and I'll get a diaper," Hattie said.

"Where's Hector?"

"She'll need some clean pants, too," Connie said.

I looked down at my lap and saw the bulge of a diaper under my pants. There was a wet spot at the crotch where the pee had leaked. I closed my eyes tight. I didn't want to cry in front of them.

"We're going to need you to stand up, Alma, and hold onto this bar. You can put your weight on your left leg." The two women lifted me under the arms again and I howled, but they made me stand up anyway. My body didn't feel right. My right leg and arm were numb and I had to balance on my left side. I held onto the bar and hoped they wouldn't let me tip over onto the hard bathroom floor. Hattie said, "Now, you're all right, Alma. We're going to take off your pants and I need you to help." She pulled my pants down.

"Go away," I said.

"Honey, you can't do this by yourself, or I would go away. Now lift up your leg," she said as she lifted my right leg off the floor and took the pants off that side. "Now I'm going to lift your left foot. You're going to have to put your weight on your right leg. It will feel strange but you can do it."

She said to the girl, "Hold her up, Connie." So the girl pushed her shoulder into my good side and kept me from falling over while Hattie took my pants off. I was wearing a huge, blue diaper, heavy with pee. They took it off, cleaned me up, and put a dry one on. Then they put a new pair of pants on me the same way they'd taken the other pair off. By the time I was sitting back in the wheelchair I was exhausted and my face was wet even though I had struggled to hold back the tears.

"I'll get you something for your pain and tell your husband to come in now," Hattie said, and she disappeared into the hall.

"Oh Hector," I cried as soon as he came into the room. He hustled over to me.

"You remember me," he said.

One strange thing after another. "Of course I remember you. You're my husband."

"That's right."

I tried to figure out if he was making a joke. He didn't usually joke with me. He gave me a kind smile, making me wonder even more.

"I can hardly move my arm," I said, demonstrating by raising my arm about two inches off the arm of the wheelchair then letting it fall back. "And my leg doesn't work. And this pain in my side! What happened to me?"

"You had a stroke, dear. Do you remember the accident?"

And then I remembered the dog looking down at me from over the rearview mirror.

THAT FIRST DAY, I was on a ship sailing over a foggy ocean. Every now and then an island would show through the mist then disappear again, or sounds would reach me but I couldn't see where they came from. Occasional things stuck in my memory: a dull room with a man in a suit looking at me over a pair of small glasses; the smell of cloves; a lady throwing up at my dinner table; Hector's face looking down at me, forehead creased; someone holding me up and telling me to straighten my legs; blaring television; a constant feeling of seasickness.

"I HAVE A surprise for you, Alma," Connie said to me my second day. "Your kids are here."

The first image that came to me was of the two children from the photograph Hector had brought me from home. But when Connie wheeled me into the parlor and turned my chair around I found myself facing two grown-ups sitting together on a flowery couch. They smiled at me. Indistinct memories of the two of them showed through the fog then vanished before I could reach them and hold them down.

"Hi, Mom," the young woman said. She shoved her long, straight, hair behind her ear.

"Hello," I said.

"You know who we are, right, Mom?" the young man asked. He wore heavy glasses that didn't suit his face. He looked very much like Hector.

"Of course," I said. "Where are the kids?" Then I wished I could bite the question back.

"What kids?" the girl asked.

"We're your kids, Mom. Do you know our names?"

"Of course," I said again.

They were observing me. I looked away. The rug under their feet was worn and there was a potato chip by the girl's foot. If she moved her foot a little to her left I would hear it crunch.

"Mom?"

"Donna and Carl," I said, as their names came to me. They looked relieved.

Some of the images that had eluded me before now came into focus and remained. Donna hugging me before she climbed into her boyfriend's car to return to college. Carl and his wife coming to our house with flowers and their new baby.

"This place is nice," Donna said, inspecting the room. I looked around also. It seemed like someone's idea of what a parlor should have looked like in the old days when women wore big skirts and men wore ties to dinner. The white lampshades had puffy balls hanging off them, and the curtains had a separate piece flung over the top of the window frame. The room smelled like cloves.

"You look good, Mom," Carl said.

We studied each other. I felt a little embarrassed at being there, as if it were my fault. What did they want from me, I wondered. They didn't seem interested in talking and I wouldn't have known what to talk about anyway. "It's too bad you're here," I said.

They smiled as if they hadn't heard me. They talked about how pretty the sky was, and how long it had taken them to drive to visit me. Six hours. Carl told me about my granddaughter, Sarah, whose name I remembered right away. They looked at each other. They asked me questions.

"How are you feeling?"

"How's the food?"

"What happened, Mom?" Donna asked.

"Well, he threw away the sandwich," I said.

FOR THOSE FIRST few days, wherever they put me, there I stayed. And stayed, and stayed, and stayed. Now, if you think sitting in a wheelchair and getting pushed here and there, is like being a queen on her throne with servants to fulfill all your wishes, you're wrong. The fact is you're more like a plant in a pot. They act like they have to pull up your roots and repot you every time you want a change of scenery. As the fog cleared, I began to take notice of the other people living in the rooms that opened up onto the long hallway outside my room. I came to recognize the residents who wandered the halls like extras in a horror movie.

There was Ambrose, the wandering man with the long chin who looked down at his feet and slowly raised and lowered his hands as he shuffled through the halls. There was the Hat Lady in her huge flowery hats, who had a big voice that she used to bark out orders to anyone who entered her field of vision. And the Siren Lady who lay on a heavy recliner wheelchair with her long toenails sticking out from under the blanket, and whose voice began low and quiet, grew to an insistent wail like an ambulance in the distance, then sputtered out to a couple sad coughs.

I got to know the staff who marched around like zombie hunters looking for ways to disrupt the comfort of the residents. Hattie and Connie were my favorites. They always had a gruff word for me. They helped me when I needed it and they laughed if they thought I was making a joke, which I started to do sometimes, just for their reaction.

Once, when I was planted in my wheelchair outside the dining room, a gray-haired lady with big round glasses, raggedy clothes, and the crazy look of one of my fellow captives, came charging past and headed straight for the door to the outside. Now, in the short time I'd been at Glen Willow Gardens, I knew one thing for sure; you could not just go out that door without getting x-rayed, fingerprinted, and who knows what all else. The place was like a fortress. So I said, "You can't go out there," just to be friendly. I wished someone had given me pointers about the way things worked. But, instead of a gracious thank you, I got a scowl and a frown that froze me solid. Then what do you know, but she punches in a code and out she goes.

That got me thinking. If there was one thing I could count on about myself it was that I would do the wrong social thing at every opportunity. I try to be helpful and I get the look of death. I had lots of time to think this over. That's what you do when you're sitting in the same spot for four hours and the only thing you have to look at is the other inmates and a bunch of shadow box pictures showing happy scenes. You start thinking about your whole life. You start thinking about every little humiliation. You start thinking about every embarrassing thing you ever said or did. About how, when you were in sixth grade, you brought your diary to school and Joey Markowitz found it and passed it through the class and everybody read it, including Craig Marcella who turned red when he saw what you wrote about him. You remember your husband telling you he doesn't want you to come to his office party this year because he needs to impress his new boss. And your children saying they're too busy to come home so they're going to Aunt Barbara's for Christmas dinner instead.

You think about how your fingernails need cutting but you aren't allowed to have nail clippers, and even if you had them, you couldn't trim your own nails because your hands don't work right. You think about the fact that, even though you always avoided the outdoors and the healthy air your husband tried to make you go out in "to get fit," the outdoors has become only a vision outside your prison window. You think about the fact that you're sitting in a puddle of your own pee, or worse, with the smell so strong sometimes your own eyes water.

You begin to think you have become invisible. Then you get mad at the staff running around and not even noticing you're sitting there like a lump on a log. So you start yelling at them. Sometimes yelling without saying anything at all, trying to be louder than the vacuum cleaner that seems to run all day long, and the birds that squawk in their glass cage at the end of the hall, and the radio in the dining room, and the moaning, crying, and gurgling of the other inmates. That's what you do even if you're like me and hardly ever yelled at anyone in your whole life. You yell because you finally tried to change something in your life and you completely and utterly failed and you simply want to die.

That's what you do.

Unless they've given you something to calm you down. Then you just look around.

WHEN HECTOR VISITED, Hattie would say, "Your boyfriend's here," and she'd wink at me as she cleared away the lunch dishes. The first time she said that my first thought was "Maurice?" and then I had to stop and think, who is Maurice and why did I think of him?

"I hope you know how lucky you are," Hattie told me. "Some folks don't ever see no one from the old days here."

And all I could think to that was, what does she mean by the old days?

Hector would usually march in while I was still at the table with my milk. He'd go directly to the nurse's office which seemed just right. No one goes to the nurse's office. If one of us wanders too close to the door we get smacked down. "No, you can't go in there. That's for the nurse." Then we'd get led by the elbow to the nearest TV blasting Lawrence Welk. But Hector was all business and he'd just marched right in and have a conversation with Nurse Morgan and when he'd come out she'd be nodding and saying, "Yes, I'll talk to the doctor this afternoon," like he was her boss.

"OKAY, ALMA, IT'S time to stand up." It was Gretchen, the physical therapist who wore her gray hair helmet-style and had a body made of steel. She was going to get me up and walking if it was the last thing she did. I fought her. Since being at Glen Willow Gardens I had come to realize I hated being told what to do.

I felt sure that if I could be left alone I could sink and sink into myself until my breath slowed and stopped and my heart gently pounded its way into silence and my soul drifted out of this painful world. Sometimes when I sat in the hall I could feel myself separating and going to what people at funerals called "a better place." But as soon as that feeling began to overtake me, someone would nudge me, or push my wheelchair, or feed me lunch, or tell me my hair needed washing, and my breath would come back fast and my heart would start working again like a prisoner on a chain gang.

"I'm going to die," I told Gretchen.

"No, you're not," she said. "You're getting better every day."

The news made me cry and I said, "I'm not going to walk no matter what you try to do to me. Even if

you beat me." I don't know where I got the strength
to say such a thing but there it was.

It didn't matter what I said. She won out in the
end. She yanked me out of my chair, stood me up,
and let go. It was stand or hit the floor. I couldn't
take more than one or two steps with my walker for
several days, though. I had to think about every step.
Step with one foot, lift the walker, move it forward,
step with the other foot. Repeat.

"Good job, Alma," Gretchen said after I walked
all the way across the room.

In addition to trouble walking and writing, and
the pain in my rib, my biggest problem was that I
couldn't stop from peeing whenever the urge hit me.
I'd know it was coming and it would throw me into
a panic. Unfortunately, it wouldn't throw anyone else
into a panic, so I'd usually have to sit in my own pee
for hours and hours (although the aides denied this)
before anyone could be bothered to help me in the
bathroom. I had exercises Gretchen told me to do
whenever I was sitting. I'd have to try to squeeze that
area of my body as if I was trying to stop peeing even
when I didn't feel the urge.

I RECEIVED A letter from Donna. It was a
pretty card with pressed flowers on it like the ones
she grew in her yard in her home outside Chicago.

> *Dear Mom,*
>   *It was nice to see you the other day. I'm sure
> with everything you've been through you feel pretty*

disoriented right now. But Dad says the medical staff is working on getting your meds figured out. Dad says the physical therapist there is very good and that the psychiatrist is a quack, but you know Dad. When I heard that you'd been in an accident I didn't know what to expect, so I was relieved to see you looking so well.

Glen Willow Gardens looks comfortable and the people who work there seemed very professional. I'm so glad that Dad can get there to visit and look after you, though. It's helpful to have an advocate when you're caught up in the medical system.

I'm getting ready for school to start because that's when the summer reading program ends and I have to give out the awards for the best readers. I'm always uncomfortable with that because there are some kids who I know work so hard to read difficult books, but they don't win the award because there are other kids who take it easy and read more books that are too young for them. I wish I could give the awards based on effort rather than on number of books read.

Mom, I hope that after you get home you'll feel like you can talk to me about what happened the day you had your accident. Dad says you ran out of gas and got picked up by some truck driver who was taking you out of town! What were you doing on the highway at that hour? I keep thinking that maybe you were lucky to have had the accident because otherwise things could have been much worse. It's a frightening thought.

I love you and I hope you are well enough to go home soon.

Love,
Donna

I propped the card up on the night table by my bed so I could look at it when I turned off my light at night.

ONCE, WHEN HECTOR came to visit, he kissed my cheek and said, "Hello, dear," and I was reminded of the young Hector fresh from Mexico standing in front of my desk in my father's building asking if I knew of a good shoe repair place which he called "fix shoe" place. He lifted one foot and showed me a pointy-toed boot with the leather separating from the sole, and I wanted to tell him he couldn't wear a shoe like that to work. I wondered who he was that my father would hire him even though he wore worn-out cowboy boots to work. It turned out he was the new engineer we had been courting for three months. This short Mexican who wore cowboy boots and brought a sack lunch to the office instead of eating at the deli in the building where the corned beef was stacked high on thick rye bread.

The people who worked for my father knew I was his daughter and they always said good morning to me and never asked me to get them coffee even though they made Tilda run down to the deli for doughnuts and coffee whenever they felt like it. This did not make me feel special. The men flirted with Tilda and asked her about her weekend and told her about their kids and vacations. I was given the arms-length treatment. Sometimes a new person would be friendly with me, making little comments about the weather, or their need for caffeine to wake up after a late night, but I never had the silky response that was always on the tip of Tilda's tongue. I'd hear myself laughing my horsey laugh and not coming up with a clever answer until long after they were gone. Mostly people just nodded and said, "Alma," as they walked past my desk.

Hector needed someone to practice his English on, he said. Would I walk to the Mexican place down the street for lunch sometime? I didn't have to be clever because just speaking English was enough to put me on an even keel with Hector. Also I didn't have to talk too much because Hector loved to talk about his family and his home town of Oaxaca (when he told me how to spell Oaxaca I thought he was making fun of me) where donkeys and chickens roamed and you could go into the bodega and find a goat standing in the canned bean aisle. He'd smile at my amazement. When he asked me out on our first date I had already gotten over the nervous twitch I got in my left eye whenever I was in a social situation.

At Glen Willow Gardens, he brought me treats, like a stuffed teddy bear, or some Russell Stover sugar free chocolate, and made an effort to be kind.

ONE AFTERNOON I was sitting in the hallway outside the dining room, concentrating on buttoning my sweater when Hattie stopped by my chair.

"Alma, there's a letter for you." She handed me a white envelope. I stared for a long time at the unfamiliar writing. Since the stroke, reading was difficult for me. I could focus on words but my brain couldn't hold on to each one to add it to the next, so I had to read things over and over before I could understand them. But even when I read the return address several times, and saw that it said, "Monroe Rehabilitation Center," I still didn't understand it.

"This isn't for me," I said.

"It's got your name on it," Hattie said. "You're Alma, right?" As if she didn't know. "Do you want me to open it for you?"

"Yes."

"Should I read it to you?"

"No."

She unfolded the plain white paper and handed it to me. I stared first at the dark block letters running at a slant down the page. Then I studied the name at the bottom. "Maurice," it said. I had a sudden image of a large man turning toward me and sticking out a hand the size of a catcher's mitt.

I read the letter over several times.

> Dear Alma,
>
> I hope you are doing fine. I am recovering slowly. I think of you often. I couldn't live with myself if I'd killed you. I guess I'm becoming a careless old man so happy for the company of a lovely woman like yourself that I can't keep my mind on my work. I was awful glad when the nurses here told me you were okay even though they said the accident made you have a stroke. I feel responsible for that. I'm out of the hospital now but I'll be in this rehab place

for about a month or so. I've never been much for
writing letters but I wanted to tell you that I'm sorry
and I hope you recover quickly.
    Maurice

I tried to bring up memories of Maurice. Were
we friends? Where was he taking me? Why wasn't
Hector with us? Did he try to kill me? If he tried to
kill me why was he writing me a letter? But the only
memories I could dredge up from the fog of my brain
were a smiling dog named Blue, the cab of a truck,
the smell of mildew and stale soda, and rows of corn
tilting.

Hattie found me some paper and a pen. She
carried them into the common room then she came
back and wheeled me up to the writing table. I
thought for a long time about my response. It took
almost until dinner time to write it down. I felt like
I was back in grade school trying to write an essay. I
had to ask for a new sheet of paper so many times,
Hattie got exasperated and said, "Alma, paper don't
grow on trees," then she laughed at her own joke.
Finally, she gave me the whole writing pad. Still, I
tried not to waste too many pages on rewrites.

Dear Maurice,
    I'm doing well. I don't blame you for the stroke.
How is Blue? Are you hurt, too? I am working with
a therapist, learning how to walk again and to
remember things. My right hand doesn't work well,
as you can see.
    Thank you for your letter.
    Alma

I folded up the letter and asked for an envelope. Hattie wrote the address on the envelope because my hand was shaking so much from all the effort of writing. I felt satisfied as I licked the envelope and closed the letter away. Then I sat and looked at the picture of children on the beach that hung on the wall of the common room, and thought and thought about Maurice, trying to remember how he figured in my life.

THE BUILDING I was in had two wings to it. The south wing was for people staying short visits for rehab. They'd go home to their families after they could manage on their own. The other end of the building was the north wing. It was for people with dementia or other long-term problems, and who weren't going to leave Glen Willow Gardens except to head through the pearly gates. It was where the Ambroses and Hat Ladies lived—the people who used the wrong end of their forks, or took off their clothes during dinner.

From what Hector told me, when I first left the hospital no one was sure my mind wasn't permanently jumbled and that was how I ended up in the north wing. And Hector seemed to think I belonged there. He liked to tell the staff every time I forgot things, like the name of his second cousin in New Jersey, or what year we visited Disney World with our kids. "Poor dear," he'd say, "your memory was never the best," then he'd smile, "but now . . . Well." He'd shake his head and the nurses would cluck with commiseration and tell me how lucky I was to have Hector to visit me. Most of the folks in the north wing didn't get many visitors. "What devotion," they'd tell me. I tried to see Hector through their eyes and be grateful.

It wasn't long after I got here that I made the horrifying discovery that we were all locked in, like prisoners. The door the visitors come and go from has a special code you have to punch in to open. Even when I knew about the code, I didn't realize I wouldn't be able to use it, that's how slow I was. When I asked the one of the aides what the code was she looked at me like I had asked her if she'd mind if I started a fire in the hallway. "Now, Alma, you know I can't give you that code," she scolded. "That door is only for visitors. You go on back to your room and settle yourself down." Then she walked off after Ambrose who was standing in the kitchen trying to open the freezer door.

HECTOR SAID IT was over an hour drive to get there so he'd sit in the lounge and relax for a few minutes before coming to get me. Sometimes we'd visit in the parlor with the flowery curtains and the squishy couches. He'd catch me up on the weather and I'd tell him about what I had for breakfast. If I couldn't remember what it was, I'd make something up. I didn't need to add more forgetfulness to my resume.

Once, after I'd been there a few days, we met with a psychiatrist. We went into an office by the birdcage. There was a man with half-moon glasses sitting behind a desk. Hector wheeled me up to the desk and he sat in the chair next to me.

"She didn't even remember who the kids were," Hector told the psychiatrist.

"Of course I did."

"Not at first, dear." Hector gave me the patient smile I had come to think of as his Glen Willow Gardens smile.

The psychiatrist was a handsome man in his late thirties or so. While we talked he flipped his pencil around his fingers in what looked almost like a magic trick. Then he'd catch himself and put the pencil down. His voice was smooth and I wondered why he wasn't sitting in a big office somewhere listening to the problems of pretty young housewives or executive types. Maybe Glen Willow Gardens was some sort of training facility for new psychiatrists.

"Confusion is normal after a stroke. Especially when there is a traumatic event connected with it," the psychiatrist said.

"Well, she's always been a bit absentminded."

"Absentminded? In what way?"

"Tell him dear." Hector turned to me.

What was I supposed to say? Was I supposed to tell him about the time I put the plastic bowl on top of the stove when the burner was still hot, and the smoke alarm went off and Hector had to rip the fire extinguisher off the kitchen wall? I'm sure there were other things like that that had happened in our house over the years, but those kinds of things happen to everyone. Anyone could forget which way the radiator dial worked and turn it all the way up instead of all the way down. And I bet I wasn't the first person to leave my credit card sitting on the counter at the grocery store when I was done with all my shopping and had gone home.

"Well, sometimes I forget things," I finally said.

"Yes you do," Hector agreed. He turned to the psychiatrist. "I feel like I have to follow her around to make sure she's okay." He patted my hand that had been clutching the arm of my chair. "And the mood swings . . ." he said.

The psychiatrist looked over his glasses and raised his eyebrows.

Hector went on. "One minute she's calm and reasonable, and the next she's crying, or shouting." I stared at the dotted pattern in the green carpet, feeling my whole body get hot. Hector leaned forward as if making a reluctant confession. "I can't keep up with her. Being an engineer, I like things to be logical." He smiled. "I mean look at how she ended up here. Where's the logic in that?"

"Well, maybe we'll give Prozac a try," the psychiatrist said after I didn't say anything.

"Nope, Prozac makes her jittery. We tried it after the kids left home." Hector turned to me. "It didn't work did it, dear?" My mouth filled with ashes. "She had a breakdown after the kids left. It's in her file. I already talked to the doctor about it. I never knew what I'd find when I got home from work. It's part of the reason I retired early. To take care of her. Luckily, I managed my money well over the years."

"I see," the psychiatrist said.

It had been almost ten years since Donna and Carl left home. I slept as much as I could in those days because whenever I was awake my insides felt they had been twisted and squeezed dry. That was when Hector hired a maid and started cooking his own dinner. The psychiatrist continued his over-the-glasses glare, twirled his pencil through his fingers, then said to Hector, "How does that make you feel?"

Hector hesitated then turned as if settling the question on me. But the psychiatrist kept looking at Hector. Finally, Hector said, "How does it make *me* feel?"

"Yes. How does it make you feel when Alma forgets things and has mood swings and you have to take care of her?"

I don't think I'd ever seen Hector so flummoxed. We were there to straighten me out, not to delve into Hector's feelings.

"Well," Hector stalled. I watched in amazement at his discomfort. Finally, after a long stare-down with the psychiatrist, during which I could hear the computer keys of Hector's brain clicking away, Hector said, "Angry, I suppose."

Now I had fully expected to hear that he felt concerned about me or sorry for me. All the things people say when they're talking about a sick person. But Hector said, "angry." And right then I realized he'd been angry with me for at least ten years. That was the crackle in the air at our home that made me afraid to touch anything. Anger had burrowed under Hector's skin and eaten away his smile from the inside.

The psychiatrist and Hector were still having their stare-down even though both knew the psychiatrist had won. Hector looked bewildered. Finally, the psychiatrist nodded smartly, noted something on his pad and turned to me.

"All right," he said. "Just because Prozac didn't work, doesn't mean nothing will. We'll try something else. Let's see how things go with the other medications first." He addressed me. "The meds you're on now have helped break through some of the confusion. You should feel clearer as time passes. I'll give you some names of people you might want to see once you're released from here. People who can monitor your meds and help with ways to deal with depression. Make sure you follow through with your physical therapy. The mind and body work together, you know." He started flipping his pencil and it was clear he was done with us.

"What do psychiatrists know about anything?" Hector said under his breath as we headed back down the hallway toward the dining room.

I FIGURED OUT it was the small things that made life bearable here. For instance, sometimes we'd have a special "cooking with Chef Frank" day when we'd bake cookies or something. Chef Frank was a pale, round-faced man who wore one of those white chef's hats and tied a flowery apron around his fat stomach. He liked to chat while he helped the residents so he was lucky I was there because I was just about the only one around who could say two sensible things in a row. I answered him when he talked, and I asked him about his grandkids, so we got on just fine.

The first time I saw Chef Frank, he was heading out the door and poor Ambrose was hovering nearby. Instead of telling him to go away Chef Frank put his arm around Ambrose's shoulders and said, "Let's go into the kitchen and you can keep me company while I get drinks ready for lunch." Of course, like most of the people here, Ambrose doesn't do much talking, but still, he looked up at Chef Frank like he was God, and I watched the two of them walk on down the hall holding hands and Chef Frank telling him about the baseball game he listened to on the radio the night before. Right then, I knew Chef Frank was something special.

The way cooking-with-Chef-Frank worked was this. Chef Frank put the ingredients into a bowl then we'd all put on plastic gloves and take turns mixing the dough with our hands. We'd put globs of dough on the trays, sometimes with a great deal of help from Chef Frank, and then look forward to eating the cookies. I liked to save the extra chocolate chips from our baking events with Chef Frank. Well, to be honest, they only become "extra" when they landed in my pocket. It felt a little like stealing but I did it anyway and Chef Frank didn't seem to notice so I figured I wasn't breaking the kitchen fund bank.

I kept my chip collection in a little empty flower vase on the shelf in my room then I ate them whenever we had a dessert I didn't like, or when I needed cheering up, which was often. I figured it was good therapy for my hands to tip the vase over without spilling everything all over the floor, and then catch the chips in my other hand.

THE NEXT TIME I got a letter from Maurice it was only a few days after his first letter but I could already read well—they made me practice every day, sometimes reading the day's news to the other residents who mostly slept while I droned on. Hattie opened the letter for me because I couldn't wedge my thumb under the flap of the envelope, but she didn't even ask me if she should read it to me.

> *Dear Alma,*
>
> *I was happy to get your letter and see you've forgiven me. The nurse here knows about the place you're at. She said it's nice enough. I won't say that I hope you like it because no one should like being in rehab, but at least I hope it's not too bad. My place sure's no Hotel Ritz, but if it was, they'd have to start pushing people out the door with a back hoe so it's just as well.*
>
> *Course now I don't have a job to go back to. Forty five years hauling stuff all over the country, and now, nothing. I'm about as useful as a screen door on a submarine. Oh well, I got a little house*

not so far from here. Near enough to my grandkids, but far enough away from civilization I can go a whole day without seeing anything but birds and deer.

I'll miss being on the road though. I could tell you stories about all the interesting people, like your good self, who I've met alongside the highway. I once met a kid who dropped out of high school to hitchhike around the country bird-watching! He had collected over 400 birds already. And stranger things than that, too. Maybe someday, we'll sit over a cup of coffee (or tea if you're a tea drinker) and I'll tell you some stories.

I have my pension but I'm just not the kind to sit still for long. I've always had a knack for making things out of wood. My grandkids all have wooden boats and trucks and whatnot I've made for them over the years. Moving parts and all. I suppose I could settle down with a shop to work in and stay busy.

My leg's starting to heal up. It was broke clean through. I have a cast up to my hip and a Frankenstein scar across my forehead. My grandkids came for a visit the other day and I thought little Alice (she's only three and cute as a button) was going to run off screaming for her Momma when she got a look at me.

Sincerely,
Maurice

I set about writing back that very morning. I didn't have to bother anyone for paper because I had kept the pad Hattie had given me. I couldn't remember what I had written to Maurice in my last letter. It seemed to me, though, it might have looked and sounded like a five-year-old wrote it. He must be a kind man to have written back after that.

I thought for a while before I started writing so I wouldn't run out of paper. They acted like you were demanding the moon when you asked for the least little thing around here.

As I was writing, his comment about sitting over a cup of coffee or tea got my heart pounding. I had to tell myself it was just an off-hand comment about coffee for gosh sakes, not an indecent proposal.

Dear Maurice,

I'm sorry to hear you broke your leg. That must be terribly painful.

I had a broken rib but it isn't so painful anymore. I'm told I was likely to have had a stroke at some time but the accident made it happen earlier than it would have. In a way, it was for the best because if I'd had a stroke in the middle of the night, I might have woken up dead with no one to notice me. Well, of course, my husband, Hector, would have found me at some point, but because of the accident, we had an ambulance there right away.

My right leg and arm have felt like wet spaghetti ever since the stroke. But they're getting better. The physical therapist is a real sergeant at arms and she's determined to whip me into shape. I think the only way I could say no to her would be if I was dead.

You are so lucky to have grandchildren to visit you there. Hector is my only visitor though my children did come one day. I receive letters from them wishing me well and all. But they're so far away and busy with jobs and they know I'll be up and around soon enough. Then we'll have a proper visit.

I can't complain about this place. They accidentally put me in the ward with the crazy folks, though. Sometimes I wake up in the morning and the sounds I hear make me think I woke up in the zoo. You never heard such screeching and grunting. One time I woke up in the night to find a wrinkled old man standing in my room, stark naked! You can bet the nurse heard me yelling. She acted like I was making a big fuss out of nothing and she ordered me to go back to bed. Of course he didn't know where he was or what he was doing, but I don't need that kind of shock. Especially when I first wake up and can't remember where I am. I thought it was Hector at first, grown about a foot taller.

My hand is tired, so I'll sign off here. Thanks for writing, and take care of yourself, your grandchildren need you.

Sincerely,
Alma

I read the letter over before I folded it up. I was surprised by how much I said to a man who I hardly knew. I almost erased my comments about Hector. They seemed disloyal. But in the end, I let them be.

"WHERE'S MY BRUSH? Hector!"

Someone had rearranged my nightstand and moved my bed to the other side of the room so my closet was on the wrong side of the bed. This was too much.

"Hector," I called again but still he didn't answer. He must be in his office with the door closed.

I got out of bed. My leg wasn't working right and I had to grab the top of the sink to keep from falling down. Why was there a sink in my bedroom? My right hand wouldn't grab hold of the bedroom door. I opened it with my left hand. Hector had left the hall light on. That was unusual. The hall was too long and what were all those doors?

"Damn, damn, damn!" I said loudly even though I don't usually swear.

"What is it, Alma? Go back to bed, you'll wake everybody." A skinny dark-skinned woman with big glasses and a white jacket came out from behind one of the doors. "What do you think you're doing out here swearing and yelling in the middle of the night? Get on to bed. Go on."

"What are you doing here?"

"I'm working, and I've got plenty of paperwork I need to get back to. You get on back to bed."

Then I knew. I was at Glen Willow Gardens.

Mostly I remember, but catch me in the middle of the night and you never know where my brain might be.

"Damn!" I said one more time because it felt good.

TODAY WAS PART bad day, part good day. I was tired and grumpy from not sleeping well and when the night nurse left, I heard her complain I had kept her from getting all her work done. That made me mad but I held my tongue. Then when I went to get some chocolate chips out of my vase after looking forward to eating them all day, they were gone. I knew right away it was the Naked Man who took them because lots of times when I'd go into my room he'd be in there—of course he'd usually be wearing clothes—and I'd have to practically shove him out the door. He was what they called a "shopper" which meant he didn't know the difference between his things and anyone else's. I didn't complain to the aides, though, because then they'd lock my door and even I wouldn't be able to get into my own room. Instead, I'd take him by the hand and say, "Come on. Out of here, you."

When I tilted my vase over and found it was empty I was so mad I yelled out loud, but I wasn't exactly knocked down by the rush of people running to my aid. I supposed that was just as well since I wouldn't have wanted to explain why I was upset.

The good part of my day came later when we were getting ready to have our butterscotch pudding. At dinner, seats were assigned at the aide's convenience and I sat at a table with three other people, including Mr. Naked. It was an unpleasant arrangement in my opinion, but of course, my opinion was never sought.

Now, I had noticed Mr. Naked liked the pudding because I saw his eyes light up and his mouth start working like he was already eating it as soon as he saw it. So, after the desserts were all handed out and the staff was starting in on whatever was extra, I stood up and poured my glass of red punch all over

Mr. Naked's pudding. His eyes got big and teary, his mouth opened and shut like a nutcracker doll and he started tapping his hand against the table top in agitation. He couldn't find the words to describe his disappointment, but I knew how he felt because it was exactly how I felt when I tipped my vase over and nothing came out.

I sat back in my chair and watched the aides clean up the mess. They scolded me for being careless but I didn't mind in the least. I didn't care that everyone made a fuss, I didn't care that there was a mess all over the table. I didn't care that I was acting like a child. I don't think I ever felt such freedom or satisfaction in my entire life.

I'D SOMETIMES SEE the crazy-looking lady who went outside that day. She always dressed the same. Loose pants, button-down shirt, and vest with lots of large pockets. Sometimes she'd carry a bucket of tools. She'd go out for a couple hours then come back through the door with a bag full of vegetables she'd unload in the kitchen. The aide who helped her unload the bag would say, "Thanks, Cara," and the lady would nod in reply. Once she smiled, but seemed to regret it right away and frowned just for good measure. I never heard her talk with anyone except if she really had to and then it was short sentences, one or two words long. She reminded me of Hector in that way. Not one to waste words. But with Hector, I always felt like he didn't want to waste words on *me*, but he liked to talk to his fellow engineers or my father. This woman, Cara, seemed unable to let go of the words, as if by opening up to let them out, something dangerous would be free to get in.

I GOT ANOTHER letter from Maurice. Since I'd already gotten two letters in less than a week, every time the mail came, I found myself hoping for another. I was even a little disappointed when I got a letter from my daughter, Donna, instead of from Maurice. Whenever I started feeling angry or miserable about my condition, I'd think about Maurice.

All letters to and from residents at Glen Willow Gardens went through the nurse's station. Letters were a big deal. The staff person would bring it to the resident, saying in a big voice, "Joe! It's your lucky day! I have a letter for you! Oh look, it's from your sister in California, Susie Mae, I wonder if she's over her gout," or some such thing. For most of the residents, the ability to read had gone the way of using silverware and brushing their teeth, so, usually, one of the staff would open the letter and read it out loud for the entertainment of everyone.

Since they didn't know who Maurice was, I didn't get the full announcement treatment, just an "Alma, you've got mail from your secret admirer!" And, of course, now I could open my own mail. I worried someone would take note of how much back and forth went on between me and Maurice, though. It wasn't that I was doing anything wrong. After all, Maurice was the kind gentleman who offered me a lift when I could have been walking along the highway until the hot sun turned me into a fat French fry. It would have been rude to ignore his letters, especially since I knew he felt so bad about the accident and all. But I didn't need to have word get to Hector or the psychiatrist that I was writing and receiving so many letters. When going to the bathroom, or taking a shower was everybody's business, I didn't need to be pestered by questions and suspicions.

Besides, Hector might have thought I was chasing after Maurice and since Hector knew the idea of another man being interested in me was impossible, he'd probably have thought I was losing my mind and trying to act like a movie star or something. Then he'd tell the psychiatrist I was having delusions and next thing you know, I'd be locked up for good.

Dear Alma,

All physical therapists must be cut from the same cloth. Mine orders me around like I'm five years old. And the worst of it is that I obey her like I'm five years old.

I had to laugh when I read your stories about the people you're in rehab with. It sure sounds like they got you mixed in with some mixed nuts. I wish I could say the people around me were so entertaining. But it's been one hell of an eye opener to be here. I thought I saw some tough sh— in Nam (pardon my French) but what do you think of a sixteen-year-old boy, in a motorcycle accident, lies in bed all day with his head wrapped up in a white cloth. His mother comes in to work on his physical therapy with him then she can barely make it to

the door to leave before her face turns red and her
shoulders start shaking.

And then here's me, a useless old man, who's had
a decent life already, truck goes cab over tea kettle,
and I'm still strong as a horse. Just a little bashing
and bruising. It goes to show there's nothing to life
but dumb luck.

Hell, my biggest problem, besides a big, ugly
scar, and a leg wrapped in plaster and covered with
pictures my grandkids drew, is that they can't make
a decent cup of coffee here. Burnt water with a
spoonful of sugar is what they call coffee. Now, I'm a
coffee drinking man. No booze, that life is ancient
history for me. No cigars, no chew, no gambling,
and no spitting, but I need my coffee. That's what
I miss.

Well, Alma, I'm sorry if I'm sounding bitter. No
caffeine to give me a lift.

But it sure puts a smile on my face when I
receive letters from you.

　　　Your friend,
　　　Maurice

The whole day after I read Maurice's letter, I
couldn't stop thinking about that sixteen year-old
boy and his poor mother. Sure, I watched the made-
for-TV movies where the teenager looked like he was
about to die of some awful disease and his mother
wrung her hands and his father yelled at the doctors,
and then the boy came out of it and won the high
school football championship, but the tears those
stories brought to my eyes were different from the
tears Maurice's story caused.

Here I was, surrounded by lost lives. Empty people whose souls had been plucked out of them and squashed between God's thumb and forefinger. The old Alma thought she believed in God, but that Alma seemed so far away now, like I was looking at her through the wrong end of a pair of binoculars. I could see her tiny self, on her tiny couch. Maybe reading a tiny book. If God reached down from the Heavens to extract her soul, he wouldn't find it. She'd have stuffed it behind the cushions of the couch.

Dear Maurice,

It's raining here and I'm stuck in the recreation room which doesn't smell so nice this morning. You know that smell? Like old people, throw-up, cologne, and lemony detergent all rolled into one. There are six people here in the rec room with me but they might as well be mushrooms for all the socializing they do. Every now and then a boom of thunder shakes the walls and no one even looks up except Ambrose. He raises his eyebrows and nods and says "Yep" as if he's involved in a personal conversation with God.

When I read your story about that poor boy and his momma, I was so sad, I cried during Hector's Friday visit. He tried to get the nurse to give me some medicine to settle me down but I said, No. I couldn't make that boy get better by covering over my feelings and it was the first time in a long time I had felt anything at all. I bet you can't imagine such a thing as not feeling anything. I can tell you're a sensitive man and you aren't afraid to show your emotions. I don't mean my husband is cold, but he likes to reason things out and if he can't do anything about a situation he says, "just forget about it. No use suffering for what you can't change." He's sensible, I know, but I could never adopt his view.

I guess I'm chattering on and on. I hope I don't bore you with all my nonsense. I sure do enjoy reading your letters.

Send my love to Blue and all your grandkids.
Your friend,
Alma

I was amazed to read what I had written to Maurice. I didn't even know I felt that way until I read it in my own letter. Once I sealed the letter and wrote Maurice's address on it, it became part of my true self, unburied and out in the open.

Even though I didn't tell Hector or anyone else at Glen Willow Gardens, I had long ago remembered everything about Maurice. I remembered his face and I remembered how I met him. It was the day I ran away from home.

IT WAS EARLY morning. I was up and out of the house before I was really awake enough to think about what I was doing or to scare myself out of doing it. The car keys were hanging on the hook by the back door where Hector always hung them. It had been so long since I had driven the car I had to think about which key was for the ignition and which was for the trunk. I gunned the engine too loud and startled myself and worried I'd wake Hector. Good thing he slept at the other end of the house.

I headed straight for the grocery store because that was the only place I used to regularly drive to, so it was automatic to go that way. I pulled into the parking lot. The store wouldn't open for a couple of hours so the lot was empty. I took out the packet of maps Hector kept in the glove compartment. All I knew was that I wanted to find a long, straight road headed as far away as possible. I-90 looked promising and I knew I'd seen signs for it when I was out with Hector.

At that hour, getting on the highway was easy. Hardly any cars at all and the ones that were there could easily go around me as I got used to the high speed. I saw the sun come up in the rearview mirror. It was a lovely sight and seemed to be telling me, "Go on, Alma. Go on."

It was almost lunch time when the car started to slow even though I pressed my foot down on the gas pedal and clenched my teeth, begging it to go. I steered over to the shoulder of the highway and sat with my hands in my lap, looking at the heat curling up from the asphalt. Hector would have filled the gas tank and paid attention to the gauge. The crows on the fence by the highway cawed, crouching and rocking like a scolding finger. I gave them my blackest look.

I remembered seeing a sign for a gas station a little ways back. I looked warily at the crows and they glared back at me, demanding to know what I was going to do to about my predicament. I figured I'd have to call Hector to come and rescue me. I got out of the car and started walking toward the next exit, wishing I could remember how many miles the sign said.

I was glad I wore comfortable shoes—my blue almost-leather ones with the low heels and the Velcro straps. None of those high heels like some women wear. Those were fine if you were staying in the kitchen, but for walking along the highway when your car has run out of gas and your husband doesn't know where you are and you might be killed by a car or a traveling murderer at any time, comfortable shoes were the way to go. Actually, as I found out after about ten minutes of walking, they weren't all that comfortable.

Not many cars went past. I wondered what the people thought when they saw my big butt waddling along the side of the highway. And me with my purse getting heavier and heavier as my shoes got tighter and tighter, and not even a hat to keep the blazing sun off my nose and cheeks.

The heat burned unpleasant pictures into my mind. Me, lying in a ditch by the side of the road weakly trying to lift my arm over the tall weeds. "Water," I'd croak at the passing cars. Or me walking and walking forever as night fell, stars came out, and the temperature dropped. Going on as my flesh was used up and my bones stuck out and I became a skeleton wandering the highway and haunting the roadside diners. But the worst image I couldn't shake from my overheated brain was Hector pulling up alongside me, in what car I don't know, and telling me to get in, he was taking me home.

But Hector didn't pull up next to me and neither did anyone else. Except for the truck driver who pulled over just ahead of me and opened his door. He had to step out on that little step next to the door to talk to me because when I saw the truck stop, I stopped too. As much as I wanted someone to come to my rescue, I didn't want to have to deal with a strange man who drove a truck. But the man yelled, "Hey. Need a lift?"

When I didn't answer right away he said, "That your car back there a ways?"

"Yes," I finally said, wiping the tears and sweat from my eyes.

"Well, how about I give you a lift to town?" He was talking real loud because I was still planted in the road. When I didn't answer he said, "Or if you'd rather walk, that's okay. It's only fourteen miles."

The next town hadn't seemed so far when I looked at it on the map. I took a couple steps forward. "Oh, I guess I could use a ride," I said like it was six-of-one, half-a-dozen-of-another.

He hopped down from the cab. Even though he was a big man, with a stomach his shirt could barely cover, he moved fast. My heart started pounding when he came toward me, but then he turned around the corner of the truck and went over to the passenger side door.

He put his hand lightly on my elbow while I hoisted myself into the cab. It smelled like mildew and cigarettes and the seat was sticky when I put my hand down to reach back for the seat belt. After I buckled in, I put both hands in my lap and tried not to touch anything. He went back around and swung himself into the driver's side of the cab and settled in.

Then he turned suddenly toward me and stuck out his hand. "Maurice," he said.

"HEAVY SET GIRLS like you shouldn't wear horizontal stripes," my mother used to tell me, "or white."

But on our second date Hector told me he liked girls who were nice and round.

Hector and I saw each other a lot because I worked as a secretary in my father's company while I tried to figure out what to do with my life. I was twenty seven and had gone to secretarial school so I could support myself but I had a lingering hope of finding a career out there I would float into and rise to success in. I had no idea what that career might be. Hector never doubted his career path. He was an engineer in the womb.

"He's a go-getter," my father used to say approvingly.

Since Hector had recently moved from Mexico he didn't know too many people. He used to make excuses to come by my desk and talk to me. He had beautiful teeth and his smile lit up my day. We didn't talk about school or work. Hector loved to talk about the universe and when he saw I had an astrology calendar on my desk, he started talking to me about the stars.

One of our first dates was to the planetarium I didn't even know we had in our town. He pointed out the constellations and I got lost in the stars sparkling in the black sky. It was magical. I bought the book they sold in the museum shop showing the constellations and telling the stories behind them.

After the children were born, Hector started walking faster and his eye for imperfection sharpened, while I started walking slower and worrying less about dust and grass stains. Hector took on the mission of monitoring my diet and exercise which, for some reason, only got worse under his watchful eye. It wasn't long before "nice and round" became fat. I took the kids to the planetarium by myself.

THEY STARTED MAKING me walk with the walker to physical therapy exercise room. My right foot would drag on the floor like it knew where we were going and it was in no hurry to get there. And the fact of the matter was that the walker was heavy. It was a slow process and by the time I'd get there, I'd already be exhausted. But when I told them I needed a wheelchair, they said, "No you don't," and that was that.

Gretchen would make me lie down on my back on the padded slab so she could roll me around the room if she needed to. The first time I lay down on the table, I was so relieved to be able to rest that I was shocked when I realized resting was not what

Gretchen had in mind. She grabbed my foot and pushed it so my knee bent and it felt like she was going to rip my leg off at the hip. Then she twisted my foot all around and tried to straighten my leg up in the air even though it wouldn't straighten until it was almost flat on the pad. Then she did the same thing with my other leg. The whole time I was crying with pain and she either ignored me or scolded me like I was three-years-old.

The more I complained the harder she pushed and pulled at me. She'd tell me, "Now, Alma, stop making such a fuss. Things don't get better on their own. Vigilance and effort is what it takes."

I suspected she laughed with the nurses about the silly things she made me do. Like holding on to a ridiculously large ball when my arms were already shaky from having to push and pull against her hands. One day I was supposed to throw the ball and not fall down, but I could barely hold the ball at all, my arms were that tired. "I will never throw a ball!" I shouted at her and then I started to lean to my right. She dashed over and caught me before I hit the floor but I had had enough and I refused to do another thing she told me to do. "I'm not running any races or entering the Olympics! Leave me alone!"

She sat me down on the padded table. "Alma," she said, "you can spend the rest of your life in a wheelchair if that's what you want. You can have people wheel you around like a shopping cart if that's what you want. Because it's going to take a lot of work to get your legs into working shape. The muscles are weak anyway, even without the stroke, and you're too heavy for them to carry you. It's your choice, Alma, not mine."

"Leave me alone!" I was crying but she didn't care.

WHEN I DIDN'T have Hector visiting, and I wasn't being tortured by Gretchen, I'd make the best of my situation. TV wasn't so fun now that I had to watch it in a room filled with people moaning and crying all the time. I found there were some things I looked forward to, though. First, of course, were my letters from Maurice and from my kids. And cooking with Chef Frank. Then it was going outside. Who'd have thought going outside would be the thing to make me happy.

I got so I could go just about anywhere with my walker as long as I wasn't in a hurry and it didn't involve stairs. I'd ask the nurse to buzz me out—they wouldn't give me the code so I'd have to catch her when she wasn't harried. Then I'd have to be careful when I left the building because Ambrose would sometimes hover near the door to the yard. I didn't know if he had any idea about what he would do if he got outside, but he was determined to try. The people with dementia weren't allowed outside without an aide. When the buzzer buzzed, I'd hold the door open enough to ease myself and my walker out. Actually there was a lot more crashing and banging than easing, but I was still quicker than Ambrose. Sometimes, I'd have to pull the door closed after me if Ambrose made a grab for the handle.

"I'm sorry, you can't come out," I'd say.

Once, I asked if I could take Ambrose out with me. The nurse considered this for a moment, then said, "Better not. Not without an aide."

Outside the air was sweet because of the lilacs bushing out around the patio. The fence running around the yard was covered with ivy that opened up in purple and pink flowers every morning. Outside the back door was a shallow ramp to the patio with round tables shaded by green-and-yellow-striped umbrellas. From there, a paved walkway ran in a circle through the small trees scattered around the yard.

There was an old bench I liked to sit on near the back of the property where the trees were bigger and the bushes weren't trimmed as often. The bench had a plaque on it that said "Joan Margolius 1921- 1999." Seventy eight years old. Fifteen years older than I was. I imagined myself living here for fifteen years. Then, after I died, I'd be the honoree in one of the memorial services they had every so often. A stranger would read a poem for me and people would cry because that's what you did, and most people around here had tears at the ready for just such an occasion. In the two weeks I'd been here, two people had died. There was a wilderness behind me with tall trees and bushes and rough grass growing along the fence. I thought I could hear a highway on the other side of the woods. From the bench, I could see the whole yard. Despite the name of the place, there were no willow trees, but there were flowers near the patio and out by my bench was a large vegetable garden. The garden had a high mesh fence around it to keep out deer and rabbits and residents, I supposed.

Because I could see only the back of the building, it was hard to get a sense of where Glen Willow Gardens was. Hector told me it was "in the middle of nowhere," which I took to mean that it was off in the country with no Walmarts around. But it wasn't quite nowhere because there was a pretty white church with a rose window on the steeple off to one side of the property. The church was small, but the first Sunday I was outdoors I saw the parking lot fill up, and lots of colorful hats climb out of the cars and head through the rear door. I imagined the people sitting in the wooden pews like a row of flowers in a neat garden. Behind the church was a cemetery stretching as far as I could see. I couldn't decide if a cemetery next to a nursing home was a sensible convenience or a cruel joke.

There was also a little house on the right side of Glen Willow Gardens. It had red shutters and a vine climbing up a trellis by the door. I half expected to see Snow White sweeping off the back porch, with a little bird singing from her shoulder. I had to laugh. Rows of flowers in the church and Snow White next door. My imagination seemed to have woken up here at Glen Willow Gardens.

I enjoyed the fact that the yard wasn't as well kept back by my bench. Hector kept our yard trimmed and neat all the time so I felt like an intruder if I ventured into it. But here the tree that shaded me had some dead branches, and there were weeds growing under my bench as if the back of the yard was too far away for regular upkeep. Also, the chain link fence between Glen Willow Gardens and the house next door was broken and coming off its post. I could probably squeeze through and escape if I were skinnier and had any place to go.

THE DAY I officially met Cara, the tomatoes in the vegetable garden were starting to turn orange. She came outside when I was sitting on my bench listening to a male cardinal whistling from the fence and the low hum of the cars on the highway beyond the woods. I thought at first she was marching out to collect me for something, but instead she went through the gate of the mesh fence and into the garden. She stood for a moment with her hands on her hips and surveyed the garden like a schoolteacher looking over a class of unruly six-year-olds. I watched her for a while because it was clear that even though I was sitting ten feet away she wasn't going to talk to me. She was wearing a straw visor and her gray hair stuck out above and all around it. She knelt down among the plants and launched an attack on the weeds.

After about ten minutes, I thought I heard her say something, but she didn't look over at me so I wasn't sure if she was talking to me or to her plants.

"I'm sorry?" I said.

"Huh?" She looked over as if she hadn't realized anyone was sitting there.

"Did you say something to me?"

"No, I didn't say anything at all."

"I heard you say something. I wondered if you were talking to me."

"Well if I said something, and I'm not saying I did, it wasn't to you."

"Oh."

She went back to her work. Then she said gruffly, "So you can talk huh? Some of them can't you know."

"Yes."

"May as well be statues, sitting out here."

"Well I can talk."

She grunted and nodded, and that was how we got to be friends. I started meeting up with Cara about every day. We'd talk or just be quiet. I found it relaxing to watch her at her work.

It'd probably be no great surprise to know that I never had many friends. Even when I was a little girl, I was shy. When I watched the other girls with their pigtails swinging and their dresses looking so pretty, I felt like I was from another planet. My mother tried to dress me up, but my legs were thick, and my frizzy hair never cooperated with pigtails or braids. After an afternoon trying to play with the daughters of my mother's friends, while my mother and her friend drank coffee, I would hear on the way home about why I couldn't laugh without snorting first, or why I had to knock things over all the time when the other little girls were so careful with their tea sets and doll houses.

One day, shortly after I met Cara, I was sitting out on the bench, watching her plant lettuce seeds, pouring them out of a paper pouch and down the neat rows she had marked off. My friend the cardinal was singing from his spot on the fence post. I had just settled in for a nice relax, when who should come charging out the back door of Glen Willow Gardens, but Hector. I gave a little gasp that made Cara look over at me. Then she looked at Hector and said, "Who's that?"

"My husband. Hector."

He was on me before Cara had time to say anything else. "I have been waiting for half an hour. No one knew where you were."

I had been outside for only ten minutes and the nurse most certainly knew where I was since she had to buzz me out. But I didn't want to protest in front of Cara since then she'd have to hear a lecture about my lack of consideration for others and general untimeliness and who knew what all else. Anyway, I realized he was just making a point. He had inconvenienced himself to drive all the way out to Glen Willow Gardens, which I was only at because of my own foolishness, and then he had to search for me.

I stood to go back inside without even introducing Cara. He took my elbow. I don't think I ever made such good time getting from one place to another, because before I knew it, I was sitting in the parlor huffing and puffing from exertion. It turned out he wasn't just frustrated by having to look for me. He had spent the entire morning on the phone with the insurance company and then with the home nursing places, trying to arrange my return home.

It was alarming to realize that he was working on hiring in-home care for me. I didn't like the idea of someone being in our house all the time and I couldn't imagine what Hector thought she would do to stay busy. It wasn't like I needed someone to watch me watch TV or read a book.

BUT AS IT happened my return home was delayed anyway. Just when I thought things were sailing smoothly in my recovery, I had a setback. The day after Hector told me about the in-home nurse, I stood up from lunch and the dining room swirled around me with the faces of old people spinning over my head. I had the sensation that the floor was rising and a plate of food was hurtling toward me. Then a black cloud came down over me. When I opened my eyes I saw table legs and the fat knees of the nurse. She was patting my cheek and saying, "Alma, Alma."

"Oooh." My whole body ached and my head was caught in a whirlpool. I put my hand to my heart and found my chest covered with a soft, wet, stickiness. "Call Hector," I croaked. "Tell him I'm dying."

"You're not going to die," the nurse said.

Two men came into the room and the nurse stood up. The men knelt on the floor near me.

"I'm bleeding," I told them.

"Where?"

"Right here." I patted the dampness on my chest.

"It's sweet potatoes, Alma," the nurse said. "You knocked your plate over when you fell."

Both men laughed.

I refused to speak another word as they loaded me onto the gurney and closed the ambulance door with a bang.

Hector arrived as they were wheeling me into the emergency room. I heard his crisp voice. "I'm her husband." Then I saw his face peering down at me, his forehead creased. He was there when they wheeled me down for x-rays. He was there when the girl put the plate under my knee for the x-ray. He was there when the doctor put bandages on both my wrists and on my right knee. He dashed out into the hall to demand medication every time the pain in my knee flashed like lightning through my whole body. Hector made sure no one mixed me up with an appendicitis case and carted me off to surgery. He saw to it that my heart didn't stop while I was sleeping.

After they finally finished poking me with needles and moving me around and feeling my wrists and knee, they closed the curtain around my bed and left me alone with Hector.

"Thank you," I said.

"What for?"

"For staying with me."

"I'm your husband. I've been taking care of you for thirty-five years. Do you think I'm going to stop now?" He smiled the smile I remembered from the front desk at my father's office.

It turned out I had a urinary tract infection.

"You don't drink enough water, dear," Hector told me after I'd been returned to Glen Willow Gardens. "I told the nurse to give you two extra glasses of water a day. You must drink them or you'll keep having problems."

I nodded even though I groaned inside. I had been avoiding drinking too much because of my bathroom problem. Now I'd have another thing forced on me. Even surrounded by nurses I couldn't seem to take care of myself.

CARA WAS ALREADY out in her garden when I hobbled out to the yard. I hadn't been outside since I had my fall two days before. I was using the large frame walker I had used when I first started walking and I had soft braces on both my wrists. I had to stop and lean against the walker every now and then to rest. By the time I made it to my bench, I was breathing hard. I sat down slowly. My knee protested against every movement.

"What happened to you?" Cara asked.

"Fell," I puffed.

Cara studied me for a moment. "I thought you'd gone home or something," she finally said.

"No, still here. Longer now, I suppose."

Cara observed me for another moment then she nodded and reached into the latticework of sticks along one edge of her garden and gathered up a handful of sweet peas that hung from the ivy. She opened the gate in the garden fence and came over to me. She tucked the peas in the pocket of my sweater. She smelled of fresh vegetables and of my grandmother's attic. "Eat these," she said. "It's good exercise for your hands."

She was right. Delicious too.

Cara liked to tell me about the things she was growing. Like black seeded Simpson that turned out to be a lovely name for lettuce. And cilantro, which was dishwashing detergent disguised as parsley. She grew marigolds to keep the bugs from eating her tomatoes. "My garden is Mother Earth's pantry and marigolds are the medicine cabinet," she said.

"I don't know much about gardening," I said. "I used to grow impatiens in my front yard in the summer but I never bothered with vegetables. Hector always said after the money you spend on buying the plants and the peat moss, and after the time you spend planting and watering and weeding, it comes out cheaper to buy the vegetables at the store."

Cara closed her lips tight and her eyebrows came together in a "v" over her nose. "That man is aptly named," she said.

I resisted the urge to laugh. In fact, I didn't like to think about Hector when I was out on my bench. I liked to be in my own world.

During our long periods of silence, I'd think about Maurice. Though I never mentioned him to Cara, I thought of him often. I'd had crushes before, of course. Before Hector, I was madly in love with the man who worked at the diner where I often ate my lunch during work. He was friendly, remembered my name, and even knew my favorite sandwich. We chatted sometimes when things were slow at the diner. He had dropped out of college to become a writer. He said he got more education and material for his fiction from working at the diner. And he made money, too.

Then, after Hector and I were married, I occasionally found myself fantasizing about the fathers of my children's classmates. Nothing serious. Just something to make me hum while making dinner.

But Maurice was different. It was as if we'd known each other a long time and I didn't have to fantasize myself into a size 7 dress to believe he could care for me. I remembered our conversation in his truck just before the accident. It was easy and fun. When was the last time I had an easy and fun conversation with Hector?

AFTER HE HAD introduced himself to me and stuck out his giant hand, Maurice said, "I could sure use some company. No one to talk to but Blue for the last three hours."

"Blue?" I asked. My feet were hot and swollen and my nose runny. It felt good to be sitting.

Maurice nodded toward a photo stick-pinned to the roof of the cab. It was a big dog that looked part German shepherd. "That's Blue. He doesn't talk much but he's a real good listener." He laughed a big, rumbling laugh. "The real Blue lives with my ex while I'm on the road."

After a while, I could tell he had a fine relationship with that photo because he didn't need anyone to do much talking. After Hector, who sometimes seemed like the only way he could get himself to talk to me was if I was in his way and he had to say excuse me or knock me down, this man could talk. Every now and again he'd surprise me though, and ask a question I had to think fast to answer, like, "Where're you from?" or "Where're you headin?" Then he'd look over at me, his raised eyebrows making furrows on his forehead that disappeared under his greasy cap.

Now, even though he seemed like a nice enough gentleman, I knew the worst of them, the folks who trapped people in their basements and ate their flesh, seemed like nice folks at first, so I didn't want to give too much away about myself. I felt loose and elastic while I reinvented myself. Oh nothing big, like I was a nuclear scientist or anything. I told him I was going to Springdale to visit my old high school friend Lucille, who "we girls always called Lu." I looked at his large hands on the steering wheel while I talked. There was hair on his knuckles and his fingernails looked strong enough to pull a nail out of piece of wood. His hands were the perfect tools to maneuver a huge truck around the road.

There really was a Lucille in my high school class. She had blond hair and wore a pearl necklace, and the boys used to fall all over themselves to get her attention. She always made me feel like I was a puff of smoke.

"We meet once a month for lunch," I told Maurice, "with some other girls from school who are still in the area."

"Friends are the cream in the coffee of life," Maurice said then he chuckled at his cleverness.

"That's true," I agreed.

"I'll tell you what," Maurice said, "I'll take you into town and we'll get you some gas, then maybe one of your friends can take you to your car. Do you know how to fill the tank with a gas can?" I shook my head, so he explained, real patient like he was sure I could do it.

"Oh, yes," I said. "I'm sure one of my friends can help me out."

We drove past a barn with the roof sagging low like it had held up too many winter snows. Maurice nodded toward the barn. "That there is where I picked up my strangest hitcher. Young boy. Not more than seventeen, eighteen. Thought he was a girl at first. It was night and raining with that cold rain that hits you like pins falling out of the sky. Well, like I said I thought he was a girl, staggering along on high heels and wearing a skinny red gown." He looked over at me to see what I made of this.

"Oh my," was all I could think to say.

"I wasn't going to pick her up. You have to be careful, especially with the ladies, you know. But she looked so pathetic, like she could hardly take another step, and no jacket or nothing. So I stop and say, 'climb on in,' and she does, and here, she's a boy." Maurice stopped to laugh. "Talked to me about

football. All the time mascara running down his face
and bare shoulders shivering. Not a word about the
get-up and I don't ask. Not my business. Took him
about five miles then let him off at another barn.
Don't know where he was going. Like a ghost in the
night." He shrugged. "Go figure."

Maurice had lots of stories and I could tell he was
happy to have someone to tell them to. I found out
Maurice had nine grandkids. He had a voice that was
almost too generous for the small cab we were in.
Hector's voice was crisp like fresh lettuce and when
he had his say there was usually nothing more to be
said. Maurice wasn't so efficient and sometimes his
stories helped me think up more things I used to do
with my friend Lu, who I found myself referring to
like that, "my friend Lu," like he was going to forget
who she was between my tales.

Of course, my stories were all made up. About
how me and my friends helped each other get dressed
for the prom and Lucille let me borrow her white
shoes to go with my gown. Now I never went to the
prom. If any boy had asked me to go I think I would
have hidden in my hall locker until he went away.
Not that I could have fit in my hall locker.

But it was fun to create a new me, and I actually
started to look forward to my imaginary lunch date
with my friends. I had an odd sense of expanding.
As if my lungs were filling up all the way for the
first time, and my muscles were finally moving after
a long time still. It reminded me of the fairy tale

where the princess has been asleep for years and years while vines and trees grow all around and enclose her. I didn't need the prince's kiss to come alive. All I needed was to get in the car and drive. I felt proud. It was a lovely feeling.

Maurice started to tell me about his grandson, little Joey, and him fishing by his house. "You wouldn't believe the size of some of them fish in that little puddle of a pond," he said. But when he took his hands off the wheel to show me the size of the bass his grandson caught, I saw the yellow line in the middle of the road take a sharp turn to the left and leave us behind.

The picture through the windshield tilted and the rows of corn were suddenly right in front of me. When the wheels on my side of the truck hit the ditch I felt like I was on that airplane ride at the amusement park where you tilt to the side then swoosh into the air. But we didn't swoosh. We kept leaning until I was pressing against the door handle and the view out my window was grass and weeds. A tree rushed toward the windshield. It fell like a domino against the next one as we came crashing through.

At first I thought one of the trees must have fallen in on me and was holding me tight to my spot, but then I realized it was Maurice, who had slid down the seat and come to rest on top of me. I was wedged with the window underneath me and the door handle digging into my arm, and Maurice on top of me. My arms were free from the elbows down but I couldn't do anything with them. I couldn't reach to the side to push Maurice off me and, anyway, I could tell I would never be able to budge him.

Hector's face flashed before me, full of scorn that I should have been so foolish as to get myself into this situation with this strange man on this highway that curved when it should have been straight. I was being punished for running off with the car and the credit card and no idea what I was doing or where I was going. Somehow I knew Hector would be the first one to see my body. He'd find me even though he didn't have a car and he wouldn't know where to look for me. My face would probably be blue and my eyes would be bulging. He'd know I couldn't even run away from home right.

I shut my eyes and waited to die. Then I heard the sirens.

Dear Alma,

I'm surprised to find myself writing another letter. I've hardly written three letters in my entire life and here I'm writing like a school kid with a pen pal. Your lady-like handwriting makes me think of the sad, tear-faced woman I picked up that day along the side of the road. Though it wasn't a good day for either of us, I suppose, what with both of us ending up in the hospital, rehab, and me with no job, I still think of it as my lucky day! How about that for craziness? Maybe it's because I have nothing to do around here but think, and you're a bright spot in my gloomy thoughts. I thank you for that.

That boy I told you about is showing signs of recovery. Slow, but it's there. He opens his eyes and

looks around. I've gotten to talking to his mother.
She's a real nice lady. Divorced with just her son
to look after her and now she's looking after him.
Her ex-husband hasn't even come to see his own son.
That's a bitter thing. I'm sure your Hector would
look after his family, even if he's not one to show his
emotions. Look how he visits you. Hell, even my ex
gives me a call now and again. We're on good terms.

I want you to think of happy things, not sad.
I think I told you already, but I have a special
sense about people. Must be from running into so
many different kinds of people on so many different
adventures. I know you were on some sort of
adventure when we met and I sure hope our accident
doesn't turn you from your course. Obstacles are
there to overcome. Don't let your spark go out!

You must think I'm way out of line giving you
advice and all, and maybe I am. A great big scar
on my forehead doesn't give me special powers of
insight. So, if I'm out of line, you just tell me so and
I'll stop.

They're calling us to lunch now. Let's see, chicken
with potatoes and green beans? Yum!

Your pen pal,
Maurice

I enjoyed the idea of a pen pal and, taking the role
seriously, wrote back right away.

Dear Maurice,

I must say, no one has ever seen a spark in me
before. It sure is a nice thought. Though, if Hector
saw such a thing he'd put it out right away. He's very
fire-conscious. Safety first!

Of course you're right to remind me how lucky I am to have a husband to visit me. He takes care of me and all. He lets me do whatever HE wants (ha ha). It's just as well, I suppose, after all look what happens when I try to take my life in to my own hands. Straight to the hospital and the loony bin! I'm like the pet dog who runs away from home only to find out it can't take care of itself and develops new appreciation for its owner. I've got my tail between my legs.

I suppose it doesn't matter, though. They tell me I'm heading home soon. Hector has lined up a nurse to look after me. I don't think it's necessary. I hardly ever wake up during the night anymore, and when I do, I'm not so confused. I don't think there's any danger of me getting up to make omelets at three o'clock in the morning. Oh well, Hector has always been careful about taking care of me.

But really, I don't think I'm ready to go home yet. I get dizzy at the oddest times, and my knee swells up like a pumpkin if I walk too much. And that's because I took a fall here a couple days ago, not because of the accident or the stroke. I guess you could say I'm moving in the wrong direction with my recovery. Who knows what else will happen? People are always falling around here. Even the people in wheelchairs somehow manage to slide out of them and land smack on their faces, though I don't see how they do it. I don't mean to be a pessimist but I could have another fall and that will just delay my release again.

If I'm a bright spot in your day there at rehab, I want you to know you're a bright spot in my life here and outside here. You have a kind and warm face

and I know you're a loving father and grandfather.
I don't know what kind of woman would have let
you go, though you speak kindly of your ex, too. And
if you think you're out of line in what you say to me,
then I suppose I'm out of line just the same.
> *Your good friend and pen pal,*
> *Alma*

"Are you married?" I asked Cara one day. She didn't answer. I was used to her silences. Sometimes I'd think she didn't hear me and just as I'd be about to ask my question again, she'd answer like she'd been thinking all that time. It made me feel as if I had said something that required a great deal of thought to give it its proper due. With Hector I could barely finish asking my question before the answer snapped out at me. And if it was the answer to the wrong question, I'd have to make do.

But this time the silence continued to stretch out like a rubber band getting ready to shoot. Cara frowned at her peas and a bird chirped at me from a dead branch overhead. It may have been a song sparrow.

I asked again.

"No, I'm not married," she finally said.

"Oh. Well that's too bad," I said.

"Why's that?"

I hadn't expected the question. Everybody knows it's too bad if you're old and not married. "Well, it's nice to have someone to look after you," I said. "Like Hector looks after me."

"I've seen how he looks after you," she answered.

"I'm not the easiest person to take care of, I suppose," I said, though it sounded weak even to me. "I don't look after myself the way I should. I'm almost diabetic, you know. Too fat, no exercise and I do love sweets. I'm not an easy patient." I was dismayed at sounding like Hector but I couldn't seem to stop myself.

"He's not your doctor or your father. Why does he have to take care of you? Why can't you take care of yourself?"

That was the question, of course. I should be able to take care of myself; and Hector, too. The problem was, when I tried to do just that, when I tried to finally take some control, I found myself in a nursing home, eating bland food, wearing a diaper, and having even less control over my life than I'd ever had with Hector. That's how well I was able to take care of myself.

"Well, when the children left, it was especially hard," I offered as an excuse. "Maybe because I was older when I had them. I was already in my fifties when they moved out."

I looked over at Cara to see what she made of this because, in truth, I wasn't sure what my age when I had kids had to do with Hector treating me like a child. She had her back to me and was jamming her spade into the earth around the radishes. At least I think they were the radishes. Anyway, the way she was jabbing, I'm not sure they survived the assault.

"I missed the children awfully," I said finally.

Cara's back was stiff and her elbow went up and down. I was glad not to be a plant in her care right then. She didn't answer so I took to studying the clouds.

IT WAS A Chef Frank day. Ambrose grinned like a little kid in a mud puddle when he felt the gushy cookie dough. It was nice to see him smile.

I had become more of an assistant to Chef Frank than a participant in the baking. I didn't steal the chips anymore. There wasn't as much pleasure in it as there used to be. I could measure the ingredients so Chef Frank could concentrate on keeping people from eating the chips or handfuls of flour. The amount of concentration necessary for some of the people to place a glob of dough on a tray was amazing to see. They'd raise an arm like a crane at a construction site then wave it around over the tray, or the table, or the head of the person next to them, until Chef Frank guided them to the open spot for the cookie. I found I could get the Hat Lady to put her dough down by tickling her under the arm. Chef Frank said I just made his life a whole lot easier since getting the residents to release the dough ball could be the toughest part of his job.

Chef Frank taught me much more than just baking. He told me about the people at Glen Willow Garden. For instance, the Hat Lady was once a painter. In fact, several of her paintings hung in the parlor. They were photo-realistic, Chef Frank told me, and I agreed. They looked very much like photos of street scenes. Amazingly, the Siren Lady taught High School history, Mr. Naked had been a librarian, and Ambrose was a doctor, of all things. They were like double people. Like the surprise flavor in a chocolate truffle. I enjoyed chatting with Chef Frank while we worked.

"Oh sure, I know Cara," he said to me when I told him I was heading outside to visit with her after we were done with the baking. "Let's see, I've been coming here for upwards of twenty years, if you can believe that. Cara grows the best tomatoes in the state."

He dashed over to stop the Hat Lady from spilling the Kool Aid jug that had been left out after breakfast. "So she talks to you," he said when he came back to the table.

"Sure," I said.

"Well, you know, you must be something special because it took me three years to get her to say a word to me."

"Really?"

"Yep. 'Course that was right after Mary died. Cara shut right down for a while." He reached around the table, picking up dirty utensils and cups and putting them in the empty batter bowl.

"Mary?"

"Her daughter. Didn't she tell you? Eight years old." Chef Frank clucked his tongue and shook his head. "Chicken pox. Attacked her brain. Then two years later, her husband."

"He died, too?"

"Nope. Up and left her."

I plopped my hands on the table top and sat back in my chair. I thought about how I had sat on my bench jabbering on and on about my kids while Cara worked in her garden. How funny Donna and Carl were as children, how smart they were in school, like Hector, how they wrote me letters and said they were looking forward to my getting back home. How they drove six hours to see me when I first got here. And all the time Cara worked away in her garden, smiling even, listening to my nattering. Did I stop and say, "So tell me Cara, do you have children? Where do they live?" Did I say, "What is your daughter like, does she look like you?" Did I show any interest so Cara could tell me, her new friend, that her daughter was dead at eight years old?

Thinking now about how Cara's face sometimes disappeared behind the leaves of the tomato plants, and how her hanky came out of her hip pocket before she blew her nose with a loud rush while I talked, I remembered the cold emptiness I had felt after my children left home, the metallic taste in my mouth no matter what I ate, and the panic attacks that would leave me shaking and panting among the shelves at the library or in the grocery store. I thought that here I was at the age of sixty-three with my first real friend who didn't have anything to do with Hector or my kids and I had not even been a good enough friend to find out about her dead daughter. I had never considered that someone outside Glen Willow Gardens could have problems too. No matter how much I wanted to change I was stuck being me.

Chef Frank looked up from the dishes. "Oh, now, look what I've gone and done," he said. "Look what I've gone and done." He patted my shoulder and tugged on his white chef's apron until I stopped my blubbering and stood up.

I went to the patio door and looked out the window toward Cara's garden. How could I go out there and talk with her now? How could I ask about Mary now? But how could I say nothing about it at all? I watched until I saw Cara come from around the front of the building and head back to the garden. She was carrying her mesh bag and she walked with a looseness that reminded me of the paper scarecrows my first grade teacher stuck on the window of our classroom in the fall. She paused at the edge of her garden and looked toward my bench then back toward Glen Willow Gardens. I ducked behind the curtain and closed my eyes. Then I took a deep breath and stepped back into the kitchen. Chef Frank was collecting the cooled cookies and putting them in a plastic container.

"Chef Frank," I said. "Could I take some cookies out to Cara?"

"Of course. Here take these two." He put two cookies into a plastic bag and handed them to me. "Tell her I say hello and I can't wait for those tomatoes."

"I will." I tucked the cookies into my pocket and headed outside.

Even before I'd said hello, Cara looked up from her vegetables and smiled at me, her cheeks pushing her big round glasses up. "Well, I thought I'd missed you this morning," she said. "Look at this beauty." She lifted a yellowish gourd out from under some large leaves. "It'll make a fine butternut squash soup."

I nodded then remembered the cookies. "I have something for you," I said. "Chef Frank was here and we made them."

The cookies were too big to feed through the mesh fence that surrounded the garden and even though Cara could have come out the gate on the other side, she said, "Toss them over."

I looked at the top of the fence just over my head. "Oh, I don't think I could do that."

"Sure you can."

I tossed the bag toward the top but it hit the mesh almost directly in front of me and bounced down to the ground.

"Try again," Cara said. "Get some loft."

I readied another throw. Cara had a look of concentration like she was ready to dive if the bag made it over the fence. I tossed the cookies again and they cleared the fence. Cara reached out but the bag sailed past and landed on the ground. "Great toss," she said as she picked it up. She handed me a piece of the broken cookies.

"I'm awfully sorry about Mary," I said quietly, surprising myself with my boldness. "Chef Frank told me," I said.

"Yes," she said. "Thank you." She took a bite of a cookie then smiled. "These were her favorites. Except we used to make them with nuts."

"We can't use nuts," I said. "Some of the people are allergic." I sat down on my bench and Cara returned to her garden. She was quiet for a while and I let her be. I watched a butterfly land on one of the flowers on the fence.

"When she was about four her grandma bought her a red dress with bows and birds on it." Cara's voice came from among the green leaves and brown stakes. "She wore it every single day for six months. I had to wash it after she went to bed so she could wear it in the morning."

"I bet she was cute."

Cara nodded but I don't think she was paying much attention to me. She talked about Mary from when she was a baby to when she died. I watched the progress of a puff of cloud make its way past her house and to the tops of the pine trees that stood beyond it. She pulled up a weed and then sat in the dirt and pulled it apart slowly. Her voice floated on the breeze and entwined itself in the fence and the branches of my tree, until Cara and I were woven in a blanket of words. Finally, she looked over at me and said, "Well, that's that, isn't it? My life's no easier or harder than anyone else's." She had a tight smile on her face, but there were tears streaming down her cheeks. She didn't seem to notice. She just kept pulling and shaking weeds, and staring down at her work as if the rest of the world, including me, had disappeared. And I sat, unmoving on my bench for a few more minutes, until the cloud disappeared behind the trees and we both realized it was time to go in.

I HAD THE most glorious morning. After breakfast, I was overcome by an urge that was both familiar and foreign. I stood up and took hold of my walker.

"Finished already, Alma?" Connie asked.

"Yes. I'll be right back," I said. I hurried to my room. I could hurry a little bit now. I was walking without a walker in my physical therapy sessions with Gretchen, but that was with her right beside me to catch me if necessary. Though, one time I thought she was right alongside me as I walked the entire length of the room, but when I got to the other side and turned to get her congratulations, I found her sitting in the folding chair by the torture table with a magazine open on her lap. I said, "Hey!" and she looked up and smiled at me like she had just played the most clever trick.

When I got to my room, I went directly to the bathroom. I still wore that awful diaper because, well, you never know. I pulled my pants down by myself, took off the diaper by myself—I didn't see any yellow leaks in it at all—and sat down on the toilet. I peed. Then I felt a shifting from within. And what do you think, but a long, smooth, not-too-hard, not-too-soft, poop slid out of me and into the toilet with a satisfying plop. I sighed a long, "ahhh." I felt five pounds lighter and as satisfied as if I'd given birth to a beautiful baby. After a moment of enjoying my emptiness, I stood and turned to admire the brown log in the toilet.

Then I put a fresh diaper on—I wasn't feeling that confident yet—pulled up my pants and pushed my walker out into the hall. I flagged down Hattie and made her look at my accomplishment. She said, "Way to go, girl!" Then I went back to the breakfast table where I had Connie get me another cup of coffee even though she had already cleared the tables.

HECTOR CALLED TO say he couldn't make his visit to me. He said a belt on the car was broken, so he was going to have to sit in the car shop all day until it was fixed. "Trading one headache for another," he muttered. But he must have felt bad about that because before he hung up he said kindly, "I'll see you soon, dear."

I thought I should be disappointed but I headed out to my bench with a sense of lightness. Cara wasn't out yet and I took advantage of the opportunity to think.

After the kids had moved out and I was groping my way out of the blackness that had taken me prisoner, it became my habit to spend the day in the living room reading or watching TV. Hector spent most of the day in his home office where he had his computer. He seemed to need to feel like he was still at work during the day.

But on that day—the day before the highway and Maurice—Hector had gone out on an errand and I was sitting on the couch when I was hit by some kind of strange energy. Maybe it was Hector's comment before he left, that my housedress looked nice. Well, he didn't exactly say "nice," he said it looked comfortable but that was like nice, and from Hector, that's about as close to a compliment as you're going to get. Besides, it was comfortable. The loose cotton was light and airy and, if I closed my eyes and spun around, I felt like a ballet dancer.

Really, though, I think it was the woman on Oprah who inspired me. She had gotten lazy in her marriage, no longer trying to please her husband, and she admitted he had some legitimate complaints. Her husband even went on the show with her to talk about how much better their marriage was since she started dressing up more and having the house clean for him when he got home.

Of course I realized a good marriage was more than a clean house and nice clothes. But I also knew little things could make a difference and it had been a long time since I'd really tried.

My first thought was that I might do some cleaning up, but that was a joke around my house. Hector always cleaned between the maid service so there wasn't anything I could see to clean. Besides, he had some kind of radar for finding dirt that was totally invisible to me, so any plan to clean would be doomed to failure from the start.

Then I thought of it—the perfect thing to do. I'd make his lunch. He said he'd be home by noon, and he's nothing if not punctual. He'd come through the door, hungry from his shopping, and be greeted by a sandwich laid out on the table, just the way he liked it. And, since he wasn't at home, he wouldn't make me nervous by huffing and puffing and dodging around me like I'm four feet wide and determined to be in his way. He'd be pleased I had thought of him, and that I knew how much mustard he liked and that he would want the low fat cheese instead of the cheddar. He might even make some comment like he hadn't realized I paid attention to those details. That would be some compliment coming from my husband.

The point was, those small gestures could be the first step in turning our marriage around. I was excited by optimism I hadn't felt since Donna and Carl had gone off to college.

I got the sandwich ready fifteen minutes before he was due home and put it on the table. Then I took the plastic flowers off the dining room table and set them near the plate to make a nice presentation. As the final touch I took out a paper napkin and folded it neatly on the diagonal and placed it next to the plate. Then I sat down at the table and waited to hear the car in the garage so I could get up and be at the sink when he came through the door.

Now, anyone who's ever sat around waiting for someone to get home so you can give him a surprise is going to know that's when the clock starts moving like the Little-Engine-That-Could trying to get up over that big hill—just that slow. I looked at the sandwich and it was as if I could see the bread getting dry.

I got the plastic wrap out of the drawer. It's always so hard to tear that wrap. The tear strip bends and the plastic stretches and stretches over the sharp metal before it finally comes off. I managed to get a lopsided piece torn off and I placed it over his sandwich. A tiny drop of blood where I cut my finger on the tear strip made a bright dot on the white bread of his sandwich, as hard to ignore as a bug on the TV screen. I noticed it just as I heard the garage door opening, and all I could do was stand there and feel my heart thumping. There wasn't time to get a new slice of bread. I lifted the plastic wrap and turned the sandwich over so it looked perfect again. Then I quickly replaced the plastic wrap. He would be pleased I had thought to keep it from going stale and he'd probably not notice the little spot.

As the door handle turned, I hurried over to the sink to wash the knife and cutting board but, in my haste to get the dishwashing gloves out from below the sink, I knocked the box of powdered detergent over and it spilled across the bottom of the cupboard. I closed the cupboard door and made a mental note to clean it up while Hector was on his computer later.

"Hello, dear," I called out as he came through the door from the garage.

He hurried past me into the living room. That was just how he walked. No matter where he was going he seemed to think he was running late. I could see him over the short dividing wall between the kitchen and the living room. He picked up the book I had left open on the coffee table and smacked it down on the table next to my end of the couch. I should have thought of that. After all, it's not like he hasn't told me how annoyed he gets by my habit of leaving my books lying open.

"Did you get what you wanted?" I asked him, to show interest in his day. I couldn't remember what he'd gone to the store for, if he even told me.

"No. The person in front of me in line got the last one. They advertise a rebate then they run out before noon."

"Did you buy a different one?"

"What do you think I'm an idiot? That's the whole trick. It's called bait and switch. I'm not going to fall for that."

No wonder he seemed annoyed. At least it had nothing to do with me. "That's too bad," I said.

He started to head into his office. "I've made you some lunch," I called out to him.

"Huh?"

"I've made you some lunch."

"I'm not hungry." He walked into the kitchen and saw the sandwich with the plastic wrap over it.

"It's ham with low fat cheese."

"My ham?"

"Yes."

"Well, I'll have to eat it or it goes to waste doesn't it?" He stood looking at it for a moment then softened. "Thanks."

I realized I hadn't gotten him anything to drink.
I took a glass out of the cupboard. "What would you
like to drink, dear?"

He took the glass out of my hand and filled it
with water and placed it on the table. Then he picked
up the plastic flowers and took them into the dining
room and put them where they usually sat at the
center of the table.

Now plastic flowers are no big deal and he does
like things to be in their place, but even so, I could
feel the ocean tide getting ready to spill over and head
down my cheeks. I told myself to breathe deeply
as I stood in the kitchen staring at the back of his
bald head. I could count his stiff hairs struggling
to hang on, like trees in the arctic. Why did I ever
think a sandwich would change anything? Saying a
housedress looks comfortable is hardly a compliment.
The opposite really.

"What is this?" he said examining the spot of
blood. He sighed heavily and pushed his chair out
from the table. He threw the sandwich into the
disposal then he took a banana out of the bowl and
walked out of the kitchen.

I dragged myself into the living room and fell onto
the couch. My housedress crumpled up under my
bottom so my thighs were showing. I looked down
at them. Fat and fleshy like dimpled bread dough. I
could hear Hector pull his chair up to his computer.
He'd stay in his room until dinner. I listened to the
tapping of keys on his keyboard. The sound was light
and efficient, like him. I stared at my thighs while the

blotch of sun moved across the floor and disappeared. Then I went into the kitchen and got a loaf of bread out of the freezer. I sat back on the couch and ate the bread, one piece after another until it was gone. I always liked how the first piece was hard and cold and the last piece was soft and warm.

Finally, he came out of his room to go to the bathroom. I stuffed the empty bread bag behind the seat cushions and looked up to see him standing at the opening to the living room. He studied me like I was a broken toaster. "Don't you want the TV on?" He turned it on and handed me the remote.

He went into the kitchen and I could hear him cleaning the countertop where I had made his sandwich even though I had already wiped it down. And his plate and glass were still in the sink. Suddenly I remembered the spilled dishwashing powder. I felt my housedress become wet under my arms and down the center of my back. I heard the cupboard doors open as he went to get the dishwashing gloves. "Jesus," he muttered, loud enough for me to hear. He sighed and ran the water again. I could picture him on his knees scrubbing the powder. It would be hard to clean since the water would only make it sudsy.

I stared at the ripples on my thighs, wishing I lived alone with my fat body and frumpy housedress. I could leave crumbs on the counter and put the plastic flowers on the kitchen table. I listened to Hector cleaning, and I imagined the stress of looking after everything finally getting to him. I pictured his face contorting in pain, his hands clutching at his chest, his body keeling over. Dead. I imagined hauling his body out to the garage and heaving it into the wooden trunk where he stored our winter boots. He was pretty skinny from all his walking and low-fat diet.

Hector finished cleaning the soap out of the cupboard under the kitchen sink and went back into his computer room. I think he came out later and got some more food from the refrigerator. Neither of us said anything about dinner. Sometimes, he'd forget to say goodnight to me. I'd hear him go into the bathroom and brush his teeth. Then the toilet would flush and I'd hear the door to his bedroom close, and I'd know he'd gone to bed. I heard all that happen, but I couldn't bring myself to get off the couch and go into my room to go to bed. The thought of waking up in our little house the next morning, and starting a new day, weighed me down so heavily I couldn't lift myself up. I must have dozed most of the night on the couch, because I woke up when the living room was lit with the gray glow of the sun getting ready to put in an appearance. My neck was stiff and my calf cramped when I stretched out my legs.

I got up and went into my room and put on a going-out dress, stockings, and outdoor shoes—the blue ones with the Velcro strap. I made sure I had my sunglasses, and my wallet, and credit card. I hoped the sound of the garage door and the car starting wouldn't wake Hector. I didn't need him charging after me as I drove out of the driveway. I get nervous enough when I'm driving.

I WAS ON my bench with another letter from Maurice. I had gone out right after breakfast because Gretchen was on a four day weekend and so my torture session was cancelled. The grass was still wet with dew, and the morning glories were glowing through the fine mist that lingered over the lawn. Cara was not out yet and the only company I had was a squirrel clucking at me from a low branch to ask what I was doing on my bench so early in the day.

With Maurice's letter in the pocket of my sweater, I felt like a six-year-old with a handful of stolen candy heading out to enjoy my treasure. There must have been something in the way the fall air was nudging out the heat of summer and the way the oranges and reds were beginning to creep into the leaves in the yard that gave me the sense things were different now. A female cardinal flew to a low branch in the tree and I looked around for her mate. There he was on the fence around Cara's garden calling his sweet, sweet song.

I was different. Somehow Glen Willow Gardens and the people in it had pulled a new me out from under my housedress and summer cardigan. I no longer felt like the Alma who was overwhelmed by the prospect of taking a walk or vacuuming the house. In fact, I thought of that Alma with mystification. What was she so afraid of? Not doing things right, I supposed.

When Hector retired he took over the small, annoying tasks I used to do. He began doing the grocery shopping because he'd remember to bring the coupons and was careful about comparing prices. He'd make sure the laundry got done and that his shirts came out of the dryer before they were wrinkled. He arranged for the cleaning lady to come once a week, and the lawn service to mow the lawn and trim the bushes. I'd hardly had to lift a finger in years and, on the occasions I did try to do something useful, I was told in no uncertain terms that someone else could and would do it better.

Thinking about this from my bench at Glen Willow Gardens, far from the couch that I now saw as some sort of shackle, I felt an unpleasant sensation. It was like when you're walking on the beach and you see holes in the wet sand and you know there's a living creature, probably with tentacles or pincers, beneath your feet. There was a sour taste to this list of things Hector took care of. I thought of Hector in the psychiatrist's office when he surprised me by admitting I made him angry.

Anger. That was it. Not the frustrated anger I had felt when I first came to Glen Willow Gardens and couldn't do a thing for myself. Just the opposite, really. I was angry Hector had taken over all my tasks and responsibilities. He had made me useless. With his hyper-confidence and intolerance for anything that did not work like a machine, he had prevented me from taking part in life.

But I could do things. Here, at Glen Willow Gardens all sorts of demands were made of me. When an aide couldn't get to someone right away in the dining room, she'd ask me to help. I cut food for people. I got the Hat Lady to put on her bib by pointing out how lovely it looked with her hat. I was the only one who could get Ambrose to sit through all of dinner. I'd tell him that if he stayed he'd have lemon meringue pie for dessert. Luckily, by the time dessert would roll around he'd have forgotten what he stayed in his seat for since we only had lemon meringue on Saturdays.

I mulled this feeling over, nudging and prodding it like a sore tooth. I had always blamed myself for my failures, but now I wondered. Hector, with his sharp elbows and quick tongue, had muscled his way into my life and pushed me into a corner. I felt liberated as I savored my anger.

But there was something more. Something I couldn't quite grasp. Like a bird in the bushes just out of sight but moving the outer branches. It had to do with Hector. Maybe it was hatred, I thought with a shock. Did I hate Hector? Did Hector hate me? We had fallen into unshakeable habits. Me doing nothing, or worse, trying something and failing, and Hector doing everything and being there to tsk tsk at my failures.

Sitting on my bench, I had a feeling of having left my old self behind with Hector so my new self could be free. As if the old Alma was still planted on the couch in front of the television thinking about nothing more earth-shaking than what she was going to have for dinner. I wanted to sit down on the couch next to that Alma and put my arm around her.

"C'mon," I would say to her. "Let's get up and do something. Remember when you used to bake chocolate chip cookies with oatmeal and raisins? Donna would help, and Carl would lick the beaters? Remember that, Alma? Let's go bake some cookies."

The old Alma would look at me. "No," she'd say. "I don't feel like it." And I'd know she was thinking about Hector. If he heard activity in the kitchen he'd come out of his office to investigate. He'd stand and watch to make sure she didn't get eggshells in the batter, and he'd advise her about how to clean up as she went so the job at the end would be easier. Or he'd scold her for baking food she wasn't supposed to eat.

"No, I'm not in the mood for baking," the old Alma would say to me. Then she would turn her attention back to TV screen.

"C'mon, Alma," the new Alma would persist. "Let's go outside for a walk."

But she'd look down at her legs and remember how tired she gets walking up stairs and she'd say, "Maybe later."

I would look at the old Alma and shake my head. "You can't spend the rest of your life sitting on a couch," I would say. But then I'd feel bad, because only I knew how much the old Alma didn't want to spend the rest of her life sitting on the couch.

By the time I pulled Maurice's letter out of my pocket I had worked myself into a froth about Hector and the dismal state of my life with him. Maurice was my escape. Just as he had rescued me on the highway, he rescued me from gloomy thoughts.

Dear Alma,

I don't mean to scold, heaven knows it sounds like you get enough of that, but I hope I never hear you compare yourself to a pet dog again. Now I love my Blue and I think he's a happy animal, but just the same, he's a dog and he's dependent on me for everything. A pat on the head and a meal every day is all he needs to make him happy. I know you need more than that. It's not my place to guess at your home life, but I can't help feeling that you've been kept like a pet dog all these years and you're ready for something different. There. That's all I'll say about it.

I hope your fall wasn't serious. I remember my Great Aunt Tilly. Fell off the back porch (too many whiskey sours) and broke her wrist and ankle. Never the same after that. Nasty old lady. When I was little we'd stay at her house and she'd twist my ear when she wanted me to get her some iced tea or something. 'Course I'm not saying you're like my Aunt Tilly. I can tell just from our short acquaintance that you're not the kind to twist a fella's ear.

Though I'm preparing to leave here soon, there are some things I'll miss. I've made some friends here. There's a man, Dennis, who was in the Korean War. He lost his right leg from the knee down, to a land mine. He lost the other leg to diabetes. If one thing doesn't get you, another will. We play checkers. He's good but he didn't know what he bargained for when he started playing against me.

*Did I tell you that I joined the army after high
school? I missed the Korean War but I did some
time in Viet Nam. No action—that was left to the
younger fellas—but plenty of trucks. I'm a whiz of a
mechanic, if you want to know, and I kept the army
jeeps and trucks operating. I'm sure to give Dennis
a stiff salute before I sit down at his table to trounce
him.*

*I had to laugh when you talked about the smell
there, and the people sprouting up like mushrooms.
Don't I know how that is. There are some people here
for rehab who spend more energy fighting against
their therapy than they spend trying to recover. It's
like they're happy to be taken out of commission
while the world goes on without them. I want to
shake them by the shoulders. But it's not my business
to go telling other people what to do. Preaching the
gospel of Maurice. Ha ha.*

*It's been so nice writing to you and talking
about life. I hope we can keep writing even after
we've both been released.*

Your dear friend,
Maurice

I let my hands holding the letter fall to my lap.
The mist had risen and now hovered in a thin veil of
clouds that let the sun peek through from just behind
me. Glen Willow Gardens seemed to give off an odd
glow with the sun lighting up its white paint against
the dark sky.

What would Maurice think of the old Alma—
the real Alma, the Alma I was going back to soon?
What had I done about my therapy other than

complain? I cried and moaned and fought. Though I was getting better, even better than I was before the accident, it was only because Gretchen was a fighter. Not because I was trying. There was no fooling myself about what my life would be as soon as I got home. The new Alma would stay here on her bench, and the old Alma would be on the couch, eating a loaf of white bread.

I turned back to the letter. Maurice couldn't be part of my life after I left here. There was no way that I could receive letters at home without Hector knowing about it. I thought about getting a post office box, but I dismissed that idea almost as soon as I had it. How could I leave the house without telling Hector where I was going? I'm sure after all that had happened, he'd never let me take the car by myself. No, once I left Glen Willow Gardens I couldn't keep up a correspondence with Maurice.

My shoulders felt heavy. I wrapped my sweater around me and the old Alma came to visit me on my bench. "See?" she said. "It's not so easy, is it? Real life's not as easy as lying to Ambrose about lemon meringue pie, and tickling the Hat Lady under the arm. Maurice only knows the Alma you made up in his truck. He thinks you have girlfriends who you have lunch with. He thinks you're a lovely lady who goes out and does things. A lady who had a little bad luck one day. What would he think of the real thing?" the old Alma taunted me. "You know, it's possible you belong here at Glen Willow Gardens," she told me.

She wasn't being unkind, just realistic. "Where else would being able to go to the bathroom by yourself be cause for celebration? I can't imagine Hector standing up and cheering when you remember to flush the toilet and zip up your pants."

A chill had entered the air. I stuffed Maurice's letter back in my pocket and folded my arms across my chest, pulling my sweater tighter around me.

"It's okay," the old Alma told me. She put her arm across my shoulders. "I'll stay with you."

LATER, BEFORE DINNER I read Maurice's letter again and I wrote back. First, I told him about the weather, and the food and everything except me. Then I crumpled up that letter and wrote a real one.

Dear Maurice,

I'm sorry to say it, but that person you talked about in your last letter is me. You've never seen anyone fight as hard against physical therapy. I have no friends. I have no hobbies or interests. I'm an embarrassment to my husband and to my children. If Hector treats me like a pet dog, it's because I act like a pet dog.

That's why I was on the highway that day. I was running away from me. I was running away from the TV, from Oprah, from the soap operas. I was running away from my bedroom where my brush and comb are laid out in the same spot on the dresser, and the same orange flowered curtains have hung ever since I got back from my honeymoon. I was running away from the Alma

*who doesn't know how to drive a car without
running out of gas, the Alma who can't even make
a sandwich right.*

   *And Maurice, we can never write to each other
after I leave here. The old Alma would never write
letters to a strange man. And you wouldn't want to
write to me. I would have nothing to say, unless you
want to hear about what's on daytime TV. Hector
has known for many years that I can't take care of
myself. He does so much at home to make sure it gets
done right. He tries to help me. He tells me what to
eat, and to exercise, so I can improve myself. But I
don't do it. I don't want to do what he tells me. I
want to be left alone.*

   *Maurice, you are such a kind gentleman. I will
be sorry to say good-bye when I leave here. I hope
you remember the new Alma, because she won't be
coming home with me.*

   Sadly,
   The New Alma

I read my letter over and crumpled it up, too.
Then I uncrumpled it and smoothed it out as best
I could. I folded it and put it in the envelope and
put it on the outgoing mail pile on the nurse's desk.
Well, that was that. The new Alma folded up into a
rectangle and mailed off.

"ARE YOU READY, Alma?" Cara held the flap in
the fence open and gestured me toward it. We were
standing at the far end of the yard where the fence
separated Glen Willow Gardens from the little house

next door. "That's where I live," Cara told me once. "Didn't you know that?"

"How could I know that?" There was no end to the mystery that surrounded my friend Cara.

Cara had invited me to her house, to play hooky from rehab. We knew we were running out of time. I could use the bathroom and walk without my walker, now, so we both knew I'd be leaving very soon. The plan was that I would sneak out of the yard and she would show me her house, then I'd sneak back to Glen Willow Gardens and no one would be the wiser. The day she pointed out the break in the fence, she looked like a kid with her parents' cigarettes. "I never use it, really. What do I want to sneak into Glen Willow for?"

I squinted at the opening in the fence. It looked very narrow. "I'm too fat to get through there."

"I don't think so."

"What if someone comes out looking for me?"

"That's never happened before. At least not before lunch time. It is a risk, though." Cara frowned as if reconsidering.

I was afraid she'd change her mind. I glanced back over my shoulder at the door to the patio. Then I looked toward Cara's house. It wasn't so far away. I could make a quick visit and be back on my bench before I was missed. It was an exciting prospect. Like sneaking out during school—something I'd never done. For some reason, it never occurred to either of us to simply tell the nurse I was leaving with Cara for the afternoon. "Okay," I said. Cara held the fence back as far as it would go and I scrunched down and squeezed through. I found myself on the other side looking at Glen Willow Gardens through the gray metal diamonds of the fence. It seemed remote and foreign.

Cara took my hand. "We'd better hurry, Alma. I made a treat for you."

I followed Cara through her yard. It was cooler and a deeper shade of green than when I looked at it from the other side of the fence. Her house, which always looked to me as if it came out of a fairy tale, beckoned.

When she first mentioned the idea of my coming to her house, I found myself imagining our visit the way I used to imagine the easy friendships of the girls I went to school with—sitting around on pillows or beanbag chairs, chatting and laughing about the boys at school, trying on each other's clothes, experimenting with make-up. The kind of friendships I never had. My friendships had been halting and awkward, with girls who were shy, like me, and who said the wrong things and wore clothes that weren't quite in fashion and that hung uneasily over round hips and heavy breasts. We were the girls who stood in the corners at the school dances and pretended we were more interested in what we were talking about than in the boys and music. But we even felt uneasy with each other because what brought us together was not that we liked each other but that no one else liked us. So, while I hoped for friendship and ease with Cara, I was afraid.

But I could tell Cara wasn't thinking any of these things. She was excited and happy, like I was a special treat she was bringing home. I wondered how long it had been since she'd had a visitor. I wondered what kind of girl she had been. Had she been one of the popular girls, or had she been like me, trying to fit in while at the same time trying to be invisible?

"I've made something I'm sure you'll like. Butternut squash soup. With cream and a little cinnamon," Cara said as she opened her back door and ushered me into her house.

I was not prepared for what I saw. Cara kept the garden neat and orderly, with her peas in tidy rows, her squash confined to one area, and her tomatoes obediently climbing stakes. But her house was a chaos of piles. Piles of newspapers stacked by the back door, yellowed near the bottom and white at the top. Coats for a family of three hung from hooks along the wall. Hats, and scarves were a jumble on the shelf over the hooks. Boots and shoes of variety of sizes were lined up on the floor underneath the coats.

Cara noticed I was looking at a pink coat with fur around the hood hanging next to a man's quilted jacket with flannel lining.

"Oh," she said, her hands fluttering nervously, "silly to have these here. I don't get around to putting things away." She laughed a short, sharp exhalation. She took the two coats off their hooks and looked around for a place to put them, finally tossing them over the back of a kitchen chair. "I'll get to them later," she said.

Cara's kitchen was equally cluttered with a small table and four vinyl-coated chairs. Sweaters and long, button-down shirts were tossed carelessly over the backs of chairs and another stack of magazines and catalogs threatened to fall off one of them. The countertop was covered with bowls of vegetables, ceramic holders and spoon rests made by a child. Small rag rugs were scattered over the floor and a rocking chair with flowery pads was by the window. All along the windowsill were knickknacks of china, wood, metal, and clay. Some obviously handmade, some bought.

"Have a seat, Alma. I want you to try my soup." Cara bustled over to the table, cleared off two seats, and carried the clothes and papers into the next room where I could hear her drop them. Then she picked up the girl's pink coat, and the man's flannel-lined coat and carried them back into the hall by the door where she hung them on the hooks they had been hanging on when I arrived. I sat at the table. The sweet smell of cinnamon and squash filled the air. There were three sets of salt and pepper shakers in the center of the table, surrounding a napkin holder filled with mail. I picked up the pepper shaker that was a clay blob painted a variety of bright colors in no particular pattern.

"Mary made that. She loved the clay class at summer camp. I have lots of things she made." Cara waved around the room. Then she ladled out two small bowls of soup and brought them over to the table. The soup was thick and orange and Cara had sprinkled cinnamon on top. It looked and smelled inviting, especially after eating only institutional food for so long. Cara put out two cloth napkins in napkin rings that looked like Mary's work. She handed one to me and put the other next to her bowl. Then she sat down. "Bon appétit," she said and we dug in.

As the soup warmed my insides I felt as if I had been drawn into a crowded but cozy nest and Cara was the mother bird, taking care of me and seeing to it I had enough to eat and was comfortable and happy. The rest of the world was shut out. No danger or discomfort could find its way past Cara's clutter.

I told Cara about Maurice. It was strange to have someone to confide in and even stranger to have something to confide. Cara nodded as if corresponding with a man I barely knew was the most natural thing in the world.

"I'll kind of miss Maurice's letters when I leave here," I said.

A frown pulled at corners of Cara's mouth and she looked down at her soup. I felt an odd urge to put my hand on her shoulder.

Then she took a quick breath and lifted her shoulders like a soldier starting a march. She smiled. "Well," she said, "you'll have to start a garden back home. Grow your own tomatoes." And we talked about gardens and birds and life. I found myself telling Cara about what I was like as a child, not making anything up like I had with Maurice, but not telling about the loneliness either. I told her about the books I had loved to read, and the tree I used to climb because it had a low branch and a root I could use like a step to swing my leg over and sit back. I told her about my pet hamster that lived for almost three years and loved to climb up my sleeves and under my shirt.

After we were done with our soup, I cleared the dishes and washed them while Cara put the rest of the soup away. We chatted the whole time. At one point, Cara sat at the kitchen table while I stood at the sink. I felt as if I were in my own home. We laughed about the block of moldy cheese in her refrigerator. "You even grow things here!" I said and Cara thought me very clever.

As we parted at the fence, Cara became serious and sad. "I so enjoyed your company, Alma. It has been so long since anyone has sat at my kitchen table." She pressed something into my hand. It was one of Mary's napkin rings. I slipped it into my pocket. I couldn't even speak.

WEDNESDAYS WERE THE days that the Footloose Band played in the parlor and people danced, though I use the word "dance" loosely. The Footloose Band was three old men who played fiddle, keyboard, and guitar. They grinned and told silly jokes. They threw compliments at the ladies and teased the men about their drinking and courting days. I liked the music and the compliments so I'd sit in one of the folding chairs along the wall and watch the show.

Usually Hattie and Connie would help the residents by taking them by the hand and leading them to the dance floor. The Hat Lady would sway stiffly and wave her arms to the music and be Gypsy Rose Lee. Connie knew how to jitterbug even though she was young, and she'd make Ambrose smile when she held his hands and danced with him. He'd even put up one hand and turn with the music. Watching them reminded me of when Hector and I were first married when we'd go to the Chester Tavern for the old-time band that played on Monday nights and we'd jitterbug and foxtrot. Hector said everyone dances in Mexico, and I'd been tortured by dance lessons when I was younger in my mother's effort to force some grace on me. We cut a fine couple even though I was fat and he was short. We quit going after Donna and Carl were born. Not sure why.

Hattie and Connie could never get me to dance. They didn't have Gretchen's forceful nature and I could be stubborn. Instead, I'd sit and watch and put my hand in my pocket to rub the napkin ring Cara had given me. There was a smooth indentation on the side just right for my thumb. It was like I had a little piece of Cara in my pocket right at my fingertips whenever I needed her.

I was rubbing the ring and watching the dancers when Hector arrived. He was visiting on that last Wednesday to make up for missing our visit when his car was in the shop. I started to get up to go to the parlor but just then the band began to play "Let it Rain," and Hector tilted his head and sat down to listen. When they started "In the Mood," that was it. Hector astonished me by standing up and taking my hand and the next thing I knew I was jitterbugging. Hattie squealed and Connie clapped. Hector still had the moves. I had a new appreciation for Gretchen because I was certain two months ago I could not have danced the jitterbug. Hattie shouted, "You go, Alma." Hector and I were the couple from the movies that goes out on the dance floor and puts all the other dancers to shame so that they realize they may as well just line the dance floor to see how it's done.

Except the Hat Lady who, instead of marveling at our grace, jabbed me with her sharp elbow and ordered me to "move it," but I ignored her.

AMBROSE STOPPED EATING.

At first everyone thought he simply didn't like what they were serving and so they made him a peanut butter and jelly sandwich. But he wouldn't eat it. He sat in his chair at the square table. The Siren Lady reclined on the other side with an aide feeding her brown mush, and the Hat Lady dug into her food on his left side. Ambrose's bushy gray eyebrows went up and down in successive expressions of bewilderment and annoyance. His hands trembled on the table top. His mouth remained steadfastly closed.

"Try feeding him, Connie," the nurse said. "His hands have been shaking so much lately it may be that it's too hard for him to hold his fork." So Connie sat next to him at the table. She put a load of mashed potatoes on his fork and raised it to his lips. He looked at her with his milky eyes but didn't open his mouth.

"C'mon, Ambrose, you like mashed potatoes," Connie said.

Ambrose jutted out his jaw and curled his hand into a fist on top of the table. His mouth turned down into a frown and his lips disappeared. I couldn't blame him. I always hated it when people told me what I like.

"Alma, you try. He likes you."

The look in Ambrose's eye told me that I wasn't going to get him to eat either, but I gave it a try. "Ambrose, if you eat some mashed potatoes you can have lemon meringue pie for dessert," I said. I patted him on the shoulder and leaned over so I could look into his face. His eyes were staring past me at nothing. His mouth was firm and his knee jerked up and down a few times.

"It's okay," the nurse said. "Maybe he's not feeling well."

But he didn't eat the next day or the day after that. The staff tried being stern, "Ambrose, you have to eat your food. Your son is worried about you and you're causing a fuss," or cajoling, "Ambrose, there will be a special treat for you if you eat two bites," or pleading, "Ambrose, you'll get me into trouble if you don't eat. Please, try it." Ambrose's long, unshaved jaw stuck out like a hedgehog. He didn't shake his head, he didn't wave the food away, he just sat with his hands on the table top or in his lap, his eyebrows moving up and down and his mouth firmly closed.

He still shuffled through the hall but he seemed more bent over and I was afraid that if someone walked past him too fast the breeze would knock him down.

After a couple of days of Ambrose not eating, I was sitting in the hallway getting ready to go out to my bench when I saw a tall thin man knock on the nurse's door. His long jaw and narrow shoulders were Ambrose's, but he was younger with only a hint of gray in his short hair. The nurse opened her door and they consulted. The man kept shrugging his shoulders and raising his palms. His thick eyebrows went up and he shook his head. Finally, he sighed heavily and left the nurse's office. I saw him later sitting with Ambrose, holding his hand. I couldn't hear what the man was saying to Ambrose, but Ambrose seemed to have said good-bye already.

I found myself looking at Ambrose with admiration as his hunger strike wore on. His aimless wanderings through the halls, his blank look, his hands rising up and down as if he were conducting a very slow orchestra, now seemed to have purpose. Ambrose saw death coming and he was walking to meet it.

IT WAS FOUR thirty in the afternoon and the clouds that had enveloped the sky all afternoon were still hanging threateningly in the sky. A melancholy quiet had descended over Glen Willow Gardens. As if a blanket had been laid over it and everything was breathing softly in sleep. I had been at Glen Willow Gardens for almost two months and it was time to leave.

I spent the afternoon watching Cara hard at work. She wore overalls and her visor, and she pushed her big glasses back up to the bridge of her nose with back of her gloved hand, leaving a streak of dirt on her cheek. She dug up her horseradish and put it in her mesh bag. She pulled all the tomatoes off the plants, even the ones that were still orange because if there was a frost they'd die. She pulled out the last batch of cilantro that had gone to seed. Seeing her pulling out the brown plants, shaking off the dirt, taking up the stakes, and trimming the parsley so it would come back another year, I felt as if she were putting a loved one to bed for the night. It all seemed like an ending.

Gretchen had told me I didn't need her help anymore. "You've graduated from torture school," she said. "Well done, Alma."

It was a matter of days before I would leave Glen Willow Gardens, and maybe never see Cara and Chef Frank and Gretchen and my bench again. I was afraid to go home. I had changed so much.

As the talk of my leaving Glen Willow Gardens had become more concrete, the old Alma had been lurking around me more and more. I'd turn a corner, maybe feeling confident and strong, and there she'd be in the armchair by the dining room. She'd motion to the chair next to her and say, "Have a rest, Alma, you've been working too hard. You must be tired."

Once I said to her, "But, Alma, you ran away from home. That was brave of you. You had an adventure."

And she said, "Yes, and look where it got me."

So I looked around at the Siren Lady in her recliner, and Ambrose shuffling through the hall examining his feet, and the Hat Lady barking out orders for pickles, or her red shoes—the ones with the gold bows—and I thought, yes, look where it got me.

ONE OF THE aides came out the back door to the building. I expected to see her hold the door for one of the residents out for a rare stroll, but she shut the door behind her and headed straight toward me. I hated to be the subject of such focused attention. Most of the time it meant a doctor was there and he wanted to poke and pry at me. The aide wound her way over the path and stood in front of me huffing at the effort of having marched so far. She pressed her hand into her side like she was in pain. She would have benefited from Gretchen's services but it wasn't my place to suggest it.

"Oh there you are, Alma. C'mon, there's a visitor for you."

"A visitor?" They wouldn't refer to Hector as a visitor.

"He's in the parlor. Hurry up, dinner will be here soon."

I said goodbye to Cara and headed in feeling nervous. When I entered the parlor there was a large man standing at the window looking out toward my bench. I stared for a moment, my heart pounding and my face hot. His gray sweater hung loose as if it were used to covering more belly and shoulders. He turned toward me and smiled, showing his strong teeth and the dimple he had in only one cheek. He took off his cap and tucked it under his arm.

"Alma!" He came toward me, heavily favoring his left side. He had an angry scar across his forehead. He extended both hands toward me so his cap fell to the floor. "Oh." He bent like a rusty jackknife to pick it up, groaning slightly at the effort. He put the cap on the arm of the couch. He took my hand and wrapped it in both of his. "Alma," he said again.

"Maurice," I said because it was all I could think to say. I suddenly thought of the last letter I had sent him and I felt a rush of embarrassment.

"Sit, sit," he said, as if I were a guest in his living room.

We both sat on the couch. He sank so low into it that his knees rose up to chest level. When he put his hands in his lap, he looked like a school boy. I sat next to him even though I wasn't sure I'd be able to get up again out of the cushy pillows and broken springs of the old couch. Maurice rubbed his hands on his knees and looked around the room, nodding. "Nice, nice," he said.

I was confused and fascinated by his appearance. Writing to him and thinking of him in his truck had created a picture in my mind of him that didn't quite match up to the real thing. Not better or worse. Just different. "Do you know someone here?" I asked.

He raised his eyebrows. "Do I know someone here?" he said with a chuckle. "I know you."

"Oh," I said. "Of course."

He rumbled a laugh that broke through the awkwardness of his being in the parlor of my temporary home, of our knowing each other without knowing each other, of his looking so healthy and happy with his scarred forehead and limp.

I wanted to say something but my mind was filled with wonder. All I could think was that here was Maurice, sitting next to me, like a phantom that had existed only in my imagination and now appeared before me. I could smell the grease from the old stains on his jacket, I smelled the vinyl seats of the cab of his truck, I smelled coffee on his breath when he talked, I smelled a mysterious, full odor like damp earth.

"You're out, then?" I said.

"Yes, yes. They let me out yesterday. Good as new." He rubbed his freshly shaved chin. "Can't go home yet, though. Got a guy meeting me tomorrow to look at my truck. Can't be driving a big truck around with nothing to haul." He chuckled self-consciously.

"Oh, that's a shame," I said. I felt the urge to touch him, to put my hand on his arm and sit quietly as if we already shared a past. Instead, I said, "Just like that."

"Well, it was about time to hang up my hat. Once you get to a point that just having a lovely lady in your cab with you makes you drive off the road, you know it's time to hang up your hat." He nodded, and I flushed. "Hang up your hat," he muttered again.

I looked at the clock. Dinner would be served soon and Maurice would leave. I wanted him to stay. "How's Blue?" I asked.

"Ah, Blue," he said, his eyes crinkling and his scar turning red. "Yep, Blue died. Yep. Guess he was playing with my grandson, Joey. Well, playing doesn't hardly say it, since Blue was past the playing age, but he was on the floor with Joey, and up and stops moving. Yeah. He was an old guy. Sure wish I had been there, though."

"Oh, I'm sorry." Tears filled my eyes. They must have been there all along waiting for a reason to come, because, though I thought Blue was probably a good dog, I didn't really know him.

Maurice looked at me with concern. "Oh, now, Alma, don't you go crying on me, or I'll be at it too." He took my hand in his. "Such a sweet lady, crying over my dog." He patted my hand and chuckled.

"Oh, Maurice," I said.

"Now, now. I got your letter. I know."

Suddenly the tears started flowing in earnest. Tears for Blue, tears for leaving Cara, tears for going home. I cried tears for my children growing up and leaving home, tears for the prospect of having a home-nurse standing guard outside my door at night, tears for the sad old Alma I would be going back to. Maurice put his arm heavily across my back and said, "Oh dear, I sure didn't mean to make you cry. I sure wanted to see you."

Hattie put her head in the door. "Alma, dinner time." Then she stopped and looked at me and Maurice on the couch. "You take your time," she said.

Maurice pulled a handkerchief out of his back pocket. It was gray but clean. I wiped my eyes and held it over my nose. Maurice would leave and all I'd have done was cry like a baby.

"Lu isn't really my friend," I sobbed. "I just said that."

"Lu?"

"Yes. My friend who I was going to have lunch with? You remember?"

"Of course," he said. "But I already know that, Alma. You were running away from home." Maurice started to lean back but the couch was never made for leaning on, and so he sat back up and smiled at me. "Alma, I've been picking people up on the side of the highway for a lot of years." He chuckled. "I bet I can tell their stories within thirty seconds of them getting in my cab. I'm that good. You had running-away-from-home written all over your sad face." He paused. "Well, I didn't really *know* it, you know, like know it for a fact. But I thought, maybe. I would have made sure before I dropped you in town. Had to see if you could get back to your car, and all." He seemed to think for a moment. "Besides, you told me in your letter, remember?"

"Oh yes, I did." And I felt proud for a moment that I had been brave enough to tell him. "You've picked up other ladies who were running away from home?" I loved the idea of a stream of unhappy housewives hitchhiking west to seek their fortunes.

"Well, no, honestly. Most of the runaways were teenagers. Not too many ladies wandering the highways."

"Silly old ladies."

"No," he said. Then he cleared his throat a couple times and rubbed his palms on his knees. "No," he said again.

We sat in silence for a few minutes. I saw the empty dinner cart get wheeled past toward the kitchen to fill up with dessert.

He cleared his throat. "My wife and I split 'cause I was on the road so much, and I didn't think much about her at home with the kids and all, and having to do everything by herself while I traveled around. She worked too." He looked around the room. "At least that was part of why we split. Who knows what comes between folks. Just different sorts, I guess."

"You traveling and her working and with kids and all, that would be hard," I said. "I always had Hector to help on the weekends. Besides, I didn't have another job so I got to do everything with my kids."

"I suppose I'd do the same again," he said. "Maybe. I don't know." He paused and looked toward the window where the early evening sun filtered through the lilac bush. He opened his mouth to speak, then snapped it shut. He held his cap by the visor and tapped it up and down on his thigh so that the cloth part flapped. Then he smacked it down and put his hand over it and said, "It wasn't just the traveling. It was the drinking. Really it was just the drinking. Drinking doesn't go well with truck driving or marriage."

He turned to gauge my reaction.

"But you don't drink anymore?"

"No. I gave it up. A while back. I never got into any trouble at work, but it was only a matter of time." He smiled. "I replaced drinking with wood working. That's how come I got so good at it. No one can say I don't put my all into whatever I'm doing whether it's drinking or making toy trucks."

"That shows strength that you quit."

He pushed out his lower lip and nodded. "Don't know that I can pride myself on stopping being a fool."

"It's hard to change your path." I gave a short laugh. "Don't I know it."

He smiled in a satisfied way like what he'd had to say had been holding him stiff and now he could relax. "Well, we all have to grow up sometime."

I hummed in agreement and we both sank into our own thoughts. I had a sense that we were sharing the space in our minds, though. It was a feeling I'd never had with Hector in all our years of marriage. Finally, I said, "Maybe if we'd waited two years or so, Hector and I wouldn't have gotten married. The time that getting married seemed right was so short. I feel bad for Hector sometimes."

Maurice looked at me closely. Then he said, "Well, it can't be helped. We do what we do."

I heard the staff rounding people up for evening meds. The Hat Lady started shouting as she often did in late evening. I had become so accustomed to the routine here, I barely noticed it until I heard it through a visitor's ears.

But if Maurice was aware of the goings on outside the parlor he didn't comment on it. Instead he said, "I like scones."

"Scones?"

"Yes. With fruit. But not like they make them most places. There's a bakery near my house that makes tender apricot scones sprinkled with sugar. You have to have them with coffee. What do you think about scones?"

"Well, I never thought about scones at all," I said. "I like apricots, though."

He seemed satisfied with this. The Hat Lady poked her head in, frowned, began to scold, but stopped and walked away. Maurice chuckled and patted his knees. "Well, I'd best be off. I wish I could have come earlier, so we could have had more time." He put his hand on the arm of the couch and pushed himself up then caught himself to keep from falling back into its soft jaws. Once he was steady, he reached out a hand to help me up. We walked to the door together. Maurice kept inhaling as if about to say something, then he'd stop with a short exhale. When we got to the exit he turned to me and said quickly, "Alma, you can come with me. You'd like my house, and we'll get a dog."

I gasped.

"Don't go back to Hector. You were leaving him. I'll take care of you, and you'll take care of me. Now don't say anything right now. It's something to think about." He leaned over and put a piece of paper in my pocket and kissed me. I walked into the dining room with Maurice's handkerchief in my hand, his note in my pocket, and the feel of his lips on my cheek.

My mind was consumed by Maurice, my thoughts swinging wildly between euphoria at having inspired the passion of this worldly, kind man and heart-pounding fear at the thought of stuffing my belongings into a bag and sneaking off into the sunset with him. I had already tried to run away from Hector. For years I had felt like a mouse caught by the tail under Hector's strong thumb. Helpless and frustrated. Maurice offered me my escape into a fantasy land. I could go. I could call the number Maurice had given me, he'd come and pick me up and we'd drive off into a new life.

"HI, MOM." IT was Donna. If letters were a rare treat, telephone calls were like Christmas. I sat on the armchair in my room, looking out the window toward the hedge around the parking lot. The clouds cast a gray shadow over the world. The small light by my chair lit up the gloom of my room.

"Hi, honey."

"So Dad says you'll be going home soon."

"Yes. Monday."

"That's great."

Mr. Naked wandered into my room and went straight for the vase where I used to keep the chocolate chips. "Just a minute, honey." I put the phone down and went over to him. "You ate all the chips," I said. "C'mon, this is my room. I'll get you a treat at lunch if I can swing it." I took him by the elbow and he allowed me to lead him out to the hall where I handed him off to an aide.

"Sorry," I said to Donna. "A shopper."

"Mom, you know what I was thinking about? Do you remember when Carl and I were little and you'd read *Who's in Rabbit's House?* and we'd act it out? I don't know why I was thinking about that."

"I am the long one," I growled in a deep voice. "I eat trees and trample on elephants. Go away or I will trample on you."

"I'm going, I'm going," Donna said in a fearful voice. We laughed.

"That's what I should tell Mr. Naked," I said.

"Mr. Naked?"

"The shopper. He's one of the inmates here. The first time I saw him it was the middle of the night and he was stark naked." I laughed. Donna laughed too. "It's a regular zoo here sometimes."

Donna was silent for a moment. "You sound different."

"Different?"

"Yeah. Different. Mom?"

"Hmm?"

"I'm a little worried about Dad."

"Dad?"

"He's been under so much stress lately. I'm sorry, I'm not trying to make you feel guilty, but since you're going home soon, I thought I should mention it. I've been trying to get him to go to the doctor, but you know Dad."

"What do you mean? Is he sick?" Hector had been looking tired I realized. Because of me, of course. Having to travel back and forth to visit, dealing with the insurance company, talking to doctors and nurses. All while I resisted recovery.

At least I used to resist recovery. Now, I took pleasure in filling in the squares on my progress chart that Gretchen had given me. It was satisfying to see how I was improving. Since I had graduated from torture school, though, I had to put my own gold stars on the line that showed my milestones.

I had always resented the way Hector lorded his superior health over me and now I was feeling healthier than I could remember and Hector was not well. Hector had always been a rock in a stream. The water, the fish, the tadpoles, rerouted themselves around him. He had been bossing me around for I don't know how long. Now Donna was worried about him?

"Not sick, exactly, I don't think," Donna said. "Maybe he just needs a rest. It'll be good when you get home."

I wondered about that. Would it be good for Hector when I got home?

While Donna told me about the kids in her classes, I was aware of that same odd sensation I had felt when I first realized I was angry with Hector. The answer was here somewhere. It was in Maurice's view of me and my marriage. It was in Cara's downturned mouth and frowning eyes. It wasn't about Hector, or the kids, or the accident, or my stroke. It wasn't indignation at how Hector had wronged me by his cold efficiency and lack of sympathy for my struggles. It was me. Here I was, surrounded by people whose lives had left them, whose families were negligent or far away, or in Cara's case, dead. What had happened to me to cause me to remove myself from life? To permit Hector to take over? My children had grown up and moved away and instead of rejoicing in their success and Hector's and my freedom, I had sunk into a mire.

I had a sudden vision of a TV science show I had watched on PBS where they showed an experiment with a little mouse in a cage that was subjected to random shocks from the floor of its cage. At first he tried to find a way out of the cage and kept trying to do something to save himself, but as every effort failed and the shocks continued for no reason he could see, eventually he just cowered in a corner of the cage and took the pain. Even when a door opened at the other end of the cage and he could see a way out, he didn't take it. He had learned to be helpless. I had felt so sorry for that little mouse I yelled from the couch,

"Go out the door! Go!" But it just cowered and shook. I was that mouse. Every little embarrassment or stupid thing I had done, or thought I had done, had been like a little shock. I had grown to believe myself incapable, unattractive, unlikeable. It was easy to blame Hector. But as long as I blamed Hector, I was like that little mouse, unmoving and hurt.

I imagined Hector at home all these weeks without me there. Maybe it was a relief to have me gone. Maybe the stress Donna thought Hector was feeling was not because of my being gone, but because of the prospect of my coming home. But now I was out of the cage. Did I really want to go back inside?

I TALKED THIS over with Cara. She got angry with me. "You are not a mouse!" she declared and I had to laugh. Then she laughed. Then she said, "Alma, why don't you come stay with me for a while? I have space."

"ALMA, YOUR HUSBAND'S here." The aide found me in the library where I was looking at the old collection of Horatio Hornblower novels.

"Hector?"

"You have another husband?"

Hector was already in my room examining the contents of my closet. "I'll need at least two suitcases," he said as I entered.

My knee felt suddenly swollen and painful. I sat gingerly in the small armchair by the window.

I noticed that my get-well cards were no longer displayed on the table but were stacked in a pile, ready for packing. I had a thrill of panic. Where were Maurice's letters? Then I remembered that they were safe inside the drawer of my night table. I glanced over to my bed to see if anything had been disturbed there. The card from Donna was still standing by the lamp, so Hector must not have gone through that side of the room yet.

Hector turned to me. "I'll be picking you up after lunch on Monday. The doctor is coming Monday morning so he'll check you over before you leave, and give me instructions for your care." I was like a mutt being brought home from the Animal Protective League.

"The nurse can't start until Monday, and I don't feel safe having you home at night with just me. I can't help you in the bathroom . . ."

"I don't need help in the bathroom." I thought of Maurice. He wouldn't be scolding me about my bathroom habits. There were some residents here who the only words I ever heard from were, "I want to go home," and here I was getting teary-eyed at the prospect.

". . . or with whatever you need. I don't need you running off in the middle of the night again. Who knows what would happen the next time. You might not be so lucky as to get in an accident and be found by people who care about you and take care of you." I could sense the control he was exercising over his voice. The prospect of my coming home wasn't bringing tears of joy to his eyes. He muttered something but he was half-way in my closet and I didn't ask him to repeat it. It seemed wise to let it go.

Hector sifted through the sweaters hanging on the left side of my closet, sliding each hanger over with a hard shove. "Seven," he said. "What do you need seven sweaters for? I wear two sweaters. One cotton one for summer evenings and one wool cardigan for winter."

"Seven sweaters?"

"Yes."

The old Alma had sunk so low that she had to justify owning seven sweaters? The new Alma reassured her—I'll take care of this. She stood. "I have seven sweaters because I don't like to wear the same sweater every day. I have seven sweaters because every Christmas for the last seven years Carl and his wife have given me a sweater." The new Alma was riding the anger train. "It's wonderful that you have only two sweaters. But I have seven sweaters, and I'm hoping that after Christmas this year, I'll have eight."

If he was surprised by my outburst he didn't show it. He just said, "Hmm," and continued his journey through my clothes. I watched his back with the sense of having been in exactly this position before. It was just like when he sat down at the kitchen table after I'd made his lunch. But I didn't feel any need to hold back tears. They weren't there.

Just as I had split into the new and old Alma, Hector had been divided. While I was here at Glen Willow Gardens, he had been relieved of the duty of looking after me and had been able to leave the bossing to Gretchen and the nurse. Now that I was heading home, the old Hector had reemerged. Had the new Alma gained the strength to combat the old Hector? More importantly, should I be thinking of my marriage as a field of battle?

I marched—at least it felt like marching—over to my bedside table. I opened the drawer and confirmed that Maurice's letters were undisturbed. I sat on the bed and considered the old and the new.

When Hector left, he said brusquely, "See you later," and marched out just like the Hector who slammed my book on the table top that day.

AMBROSE DIED DURING the night. I woke to the subdued sound of the night nurse and the aide fussing about their business. Once, I thought I heard someone running lightly past my door. Then there were the sounds of male voices, less quiet, not so concerned about waking the residents. I got out of bed, and after catching my balance on the doorknob to the closet, I peeked out my door into the well-lit hallway in time to see the gurney get wheeled out of Ambrose's room with his frail body outlined under the white sheet.

The nurse noticed me as she walked by. "It's all right, Alma, go on back to bed."

I watched Ambrose get wheeled around the corner and then I took the nurse's advice and went back to bed.

HECTOR SKIPPED HIS Sunday visit, saying that since I was coming home the next day, he felt his time was better spent getting ready. It was just as well, since Ambrose's memorial service was planned for Sunday and Hector didn't know Ambrose except as the man who hovered by the door when he was trying to leave. After I got off the phone with Hector I pulled the piece of paper Maurice had given me out of my pocket and studied it.

Sunday morning before breakfast I saw Ambrose's son talking with the nurse. Then he and his wife packed up Ambrose's things. By the end of breakfast, the room was emptied of all sign of him and was being prepared for a new occupant. I asked his son if I could have the picture of Ambrose that hung outside his door. It showed him in late middle age, sitting in an armchair with a small brown dog in his lap. He was smiling at the camera and his eyes were alert and lively. His son said "thank you" when he handed me the picture and I was sorry I had done nothing to deserve his gratitude.

Since the memorial service was scheduled for lunchtime, I was able to go out to my bench for my usual morning visit with Cara. I played with the napkin ring nestled in my pocket with Maurice's handkerchief. Cara pulled out the stakes for the two tomato plants that had stopped producing fruit, and rolled up the lattice the sweet peas had clung to. "Some things will keep on producing up to the first frost," she said. "That's why I plant in shifts. That way, there's always something getting ripe all the time. But it's too late to plant a new batch now."

"I've learned a lot from you," I said.

Cara began cutting the marigolds that remained on the browning plants. She collected them in a small bouquet. "So, the funeral is today, is it?" she said.

"Yes. After lunch."

She handed me the bouquet of sharp-smelling marigolds. "Take these with you," she said. "They're Mary's favorites."

"Yes. I will," I said. "Thank you."

We sat and talked and planned until it was time for me to get ready for Ambrose's service.

THE DINING ROOM was as pretty as I'd ever seen it. There were white table cloths and vases with real flowers on all the tables, and the sun streamed in through the sheer curtains. I asked for a glass of water for Cara's marigolds. Lively violin music was playing in the background, and the Hat Lady seemed to have decided to test how much noise she could make during the brief readings.

Ambrose's son and his family were there. Chef Frank was there, too. I read a poem out loud about daffodils that had words in it like "jocund" and "oft." Ambrose's grandson read a letter Ambrose had sent him many years ago. The letter was kind, wishing the boy well in college and reminding him to study hard but to be sure to get out to a movie or to the park now and then and to find a nice girl to marry.

Since it was nice out they decided to turn his burial into an outing, so they got us all bundled up for the outdoors. They hauled out the people in their wheelchairs, and with their walkers, and they put us on the bus to go down the driveway, turn left on the street and head up into the next driveway. Then we all unpiled out of the bus. We maybe traveled a quarter of a mile and it probably took an hour to get everybody on the bus and then off again. The complaining was fierce. "Ooh, my leg!" or " I want to watch my stories on television," or "it's too cold," or "it's too hot." Everything an ordeal.

While the minister spoke, Chef Frank took my arm. "I'll show you where to put the marigolds," he said. We walked along the path that wound away from the church and Ambrose's open grave. The stone was small and plain, but it looked pretty in the shade of a young tree whose branches flowed out from the center of the trunk and wept down in a canopy. Chef Frank put a bouquet of flowers from the tables in the dining room on the headstone. I read the etching on the headstone, "Mary 1975-1983," and underneath that it said "Beloved daughter of Cara and Joseph Hopper." I put the marigolds next to Chef Frank's bouquet. I thought about putting the napkin ring with the flowers. It seemed like a way of saying thank you to Cara. But I found I couldn't part with it. We walked back to Ambrose's service in time to sing "Guide Me, O Thou Great Redeemer."

I hummed the tune all the time it took to drive back to the nursing home and unpack us all. I hummed it while I went through my few belongings and while I wrote a note to Hector.

> Dear Hector,
>
> You will be surprised to get this note, I think, but maybe not too sad about it. You have been a good husband, in your way, and I've tried to be a good wife, but I know I haven't always succeeded. I don't need to tell you to take good care of yourself, because you always do and I know you always will. I'm glad you taught the kids to have your self-discipline instead of my lazy nature.
>
> All my best,
> Alma

I studied this letter for a long, long, time. Then I wrote another letter.

> Dear Maurice,
>
> I don't know where to send this letter so I'll leave it with Hattie and maybe you'll pick it up or she'll find you for me. By the time you get it I'll have left Glen Willow Gardens, but I won't have gone far. My good friend, Cara, offered me a place in her home and I have decided to accept her offer, at least for the time being.
>
> Maurice, I have to thank you for picking me up that day. My stay here and our letters have been part of the journey I was making that day we met.
>
> When you made your kind offer to me the other day, it was another step in finding the Alma I really am (though, I have to admit, even the real Alma

can't expect any offers as sweet and generous as yours). I don't know what will happen now, but I know I have to give myself a chance to continue to grow and enjoy life.

You and I are both beginning new adventures. I hope when you get this letter you'll respond and we can still be pen pals. I would like to know what you're making in your wood shop and how many deer you see in your yard. I hope we will see each other again.

Now I'll go find Hattie and ask her to get this letter to you. She may be bossy but she's trustworthy.

Your good friend and pen pal,

Alma

At five on Sunday afternoon I was out on my bench, sitting next to my tree and looking toward the patio by the back door of Glen Willow Gardens. I thought of the people inside the building and smiled. No one questioned my going outside at that unusual time. They didn't pay much attention to me these days. The staff knew I was scheduled to go home the next day and they were itching to clean out my room and move the next person in.

The old Alma came to visit me. When I turned my head, there she was sitting next to me on the bench with a secret smile on her face. The fearful look that had settled in her forehead over the past ten years or so was smoothed over. A light breeze blew her gray hair so it flattened out on one side. Her plastic-rimmed glasses were askew. One thick sock was gathered in folds around her ankle. Her hands rested in her lap and I could see her plain gold wedding band.

"You know," she said so quietly I could hardly hear her. Her voice seemed to come in on the light breeze, or through the leaves of the tree above our heads. "There was a time, when the kids were little, that I did everything for them. I got them where they needed to go. I made sure they had their school projects, and their lunches. I bought them new clothes when they outgrew the old ones. They came to me when they fell off the swing, or had a fight over who got the last cupcake. I made dinner and had it ready when Hector got home, and then we all ate it."

"I remember," I said.

She nodded while her fingers played with the edge of her sweater.

We sat for a few more minutes, not talking. We turned to watch as two squirrels chased each other in circles over the lawn and then up the trunk of the tree that shaded the bench. We looked up at the screech of a hawk overhead, and we watched it circle lazily down to the tree line, where it disappeared. I put my hand over the Old Alma's warm hands where they lay on her lap, and kept it there until it was time for me to go back inside. Then I leaned over and kissed her cheek. "Good-bye," I said and stood. I went into my room and pulled out the two suitcases Hector had brought for me. I tucked Maurice's letters into the secret bottom of one of them, then packed all my belongings.

Cara met me at the entrance to the residence. I didn't need to sneak through the fence. Hattie and

Connie kissed me and told me to be a good girl and never come back except to visit. Cara took my hand and we walked out into the sunshine.

Lisa Julin Sharon's stories have appeared in *Ploughshares, Sequestrum, Cleaver Magazine*, and *The Painted Bride Quarterly*, among others. This novella grew out of many hours visiting parents in nursing homes where she developed an appreciation for the humor, strength, and sadness of people facing loss of independence at the end of their lives. Lisa holds a law degree and a Master's in English. She writes from her home in Cleveland Hts., Ohio.